THE XENON TECH ARCHIVES

FILE 2:

"THE HYBRID THEORY"

BY: ASHLEY M. JACKSON

Copyright @ 2018 The Xenon Tech Archives File: 2 The Hybrid Theory by Ashley M. Jackson

3Seats Publishing
Virginia Beach, VA 23462
3Seatspublishing@gmail.com

Cover Illustration by Stanley Barros
Cover and Book design by 3Seats Publishing
Editing thru 3Seats Publishing

ISBN 13: 978-0-9986303-2-8
ISBN # for eBook: pending
LCCN: 2018914970

First Edition January 2019
Printed in the USA by Lulu, Inc. of Raleigh, NC 27607

TABLE OF CONTENTS

*** *Recap*

WHAT HAPPENED IN LAST BOOK?

Our young and self-proclaimed Captain Scarlet has left home in an attempt to fulfill his life's work by assassinating Lord Salem. Fueled with determination to find father and save what's left of humankind, he has promised Emme a safer world and has begun his journey as a true rebel.

Along the way he has met and recruited; Faylin- a strange and stoic humanoid, Tyrinie- the young and arrogant animal fusion, Casteri- Tyrinie's mature and intellectual best friend and Lanker- the overconfident geological genius. Their rocky start, along with some help from *R*, leads the team to the discovery of Salem's powerhouses.

Scarlet and the team have made their first move to the fortress in the capital of the Western region. However once they are inside, they realize that their road might not be as smooth as they thought it would be.

DOWN THE RABBIT HOLE

The space was dark and tight down in the shaft, but Faylin was right about it being discreet.

"Alright, is everyone in?" I began to crawl my way through the tunnel. I couldn't even see ahead of myself.

"We're good over here, Cap!" Lanker shouted over the earpiece. "Tyrinie and I are in the air vent."

"Idiot, I can talk for myself. We're fine over here." Tyrinie added between static.

The shaft I was in opened, leading to a walkway filled with pipes and wires with the grated floor above me. Nobody would notice me down here, given I don't trip over anything.

"Everything is clear on this end, Mr. Scarlet." Faylin added.

"This place is oddly deserted. I would imagine wall to wall security." Casteri was right, it was oddly quiet. I hadn't even seen anyone above me.

"Remember everyone; we are looking for anything of importance. Anything could possibly be a weak spot in this place."

"Aye Aye" Everyone whispered in response.

I clutched my sword to my hip, being careful to shuffle over the various pipes that lay on the floor. Thankfully the pipe shaft was deep enough for me to walk upright through; crawling over this would have been hell.

There was a split in the path; one went downwards with fewer wires and one continued forward with more wires in place. More wires meant more CHEM power being pumped in, right? "Fay, following the majority of wires should lead me to a more powerful wing of this place, right?"

"That sounds logical, Captain."

Great, it looked like I knew where I was going. I ran off following the bulky wires, dodging the loose metal and jutting pipes.

This tunnel seemed endless; I know I'd been walking for at least twenty minutes or so.

"I see some guards, Cap." Lanker whispered. "They're right below us. Permission to take them out"

I was about to say "no", but Faylin beat me to it. "They are most likely combat humanoids, I would recommend avoiding contact."

It would make sense for this place to be crawling with combat humanoids. The last time I came in close contact with them was during my little sprint with Faylin on the Southern region bridge.

"Fay's right. Stay away for now. We don't attack until we are in a bigger group."

Tyrinie and Lanker are only two people, and that wouldn't nearly be enough to take down a group of combat humanoids.

"Well we're going to have to change our path; the vent is blocked off from here."

There was more shuffling and crackling on their end before Tyrinie's voice whispered through.

"We're on the ground now; heading outside was the only way to avoid the guards."

My heart began to race a bit, they seemed pretty pinned down.

"Alright Tyrinie and Lanker, take the outside route, keep your heads down, and stay close to shadowed places. Stay out of sight." They can do this; those two are the stealthiest after all.

"Gotcha, Cap."

2

The two of them went silent as I focused ahead. The area was brighter; the CHEM from the pipe below was glowing a deep blue, casting everything in a dark shadow. The wires were thicker and outlined the entire chute.

"Anything on your end, Casteri?" I asked, making another left. Nothing...

"Casteri, Faylin, you guys alright?"

I paused, about to call out again before Casteri's voice came through in a whisper. "We are in view of a door, first one we've seen guarded in the last half hour."

"Only guarded by two men, humans certainly, we can take them Mr. Scarlet." Faylin added in.

I paused, my eyes caught by a strange green glow. Looking up through a grate in the tunnel, I saw two familiar silhouettes.

"Faylin, Casteri, I'm right under you guys." I didn't understand why things seemed strange until it clicked. The glow was coming from green sparks that traveled up and down Faylin's hands. It was all too similar to mine.

"Did you hear me, Captain?" Casteri's voice broke my thoughts. I jumped and shook my head. "Repeat. I didn't catch that."

"Permission for us to proceed forward into the guarded room?" I looked ahead at what appeared to be a dead end as well. Low and behold, the majority of the wires seemed to pour into the room.

"Permission granted I'll be making my way there as well. Be careful you two." Now I just needed to find my own way out of this tunnel.

There was a metal grate overhead, it seemed loose enough. The walls were slick, but there were wires covering the tunnel walls from top to bottom, looks like I found my way up.

I stretched out my fingers, bathing them in their normal red glow, as I wrapped both hands around a thicker wire and hoisted myself up with a familiar ease. Looked like all those years of climbing trees finally came in handy.

I made my way up to the grate above me and secured my hands tightly in the wires. There was a good chance that I only had one shot to make it work. I loosened my legs so that I was dangling from my hands, before swinging back and forth, slamming both legs full force into the grate lid. A loud clang sounded as the cover was pushed up and aside.

It actually worked.

I smiled in triumph as I reached the opening and pulled myself out of the pipe shaft. By the time I reached the surface, both guards were out cold, lying tied up in the corner of the now jarred doorway. Fay and Casteri sure made quick work out of those guys.

"It's me you two." I pushed my way in, shutting the door behind me. Faylin was typing on the computer's hologram, which had at least seven different screens of different sizes and three keyboards, while Casteri was sorting through files and papers, tossing most on the floor, but holding on to quite a few.

"What have I missed?" I stood behind Faylin, taking a look around the massive computer room.

Faylin looked around each of the screens, seeming just as confused as me. "I just got into the database, but all I have found are messages with no name as a sender. Each sender seems to be under the same codeword: Management."

Management? That's odd.

"Management?" Casteri popped up from the file he was in, coming over to us. "Bring up everything you have on *Management*. I might have something."

He dumped a stack of papers on the desk, spreading them out in some weird order.

I peered closer, trying to decipher what was there. The messages were orders sent to and from "Management".

A number seemed to accompany the word "Management", like "Management 1" and "Management 2".

"Perhaps *Management* is, a who and not a what." Casteri pointed out before all of our earpieces crackled to life.

"Hey, where are you guys? We're still in this courtyard." Lanker's voice came through in a bit of a panic. "This storm is picking up, so we should get inside ASAP, Cap."

I almost forgot all about the storm!

"Hang on you two let me get to a window." I sped off back to the door, "Faylin and Casteri, you both stay here and keep looking up what you found."

I headed back into the hallway and straight for the closest opening. I needed a landmark, something to give Lanker.

"Lanker, can you hear me." I could only hope this would work, after all, he was good at directions.

"Loud and clear, Cap."

"Okay." I squinted through the dirt swirling outside the window. "Clock tower. There's a clock tower that you should see."

"Okay, yea we see that!"

"Okay, starting from the front of the tower, we are in the hallway about 15 degrees northwest, fourth level up. Got that?"

It was quiet for a moment before I heard Lanker chuckling. "Got it, be there in five minutes."

I let out a sigh of relief; at least they were taken care of.

I walked back into the computer room where Fay and Casteri were crowded around new images that appeared above the keyboard. They looked like messages, or maybe even letters.

"What did we find?" The set of messages seemed to be from Management 4 being sent to Management 3. Then there was one from Management 4 again, but this time being sent to Management 1.

"Who's Management?" I grabbed some of the papers Casteri had pulled from earlier.

Sure enough, Management was a "who" and not a "what". There seemed to be a lot of them, but how did this tie in with Salem?

The door opened and a very wet Tyrinie and Lanker trudged in. Lanker gave a wave while ringing out his coat. "That storm is picking up Cap. What's going on?"

Tyrinie rung out the corners of his cloak before closing the door and heading over as well. We were all together and safe for the time being. At least now we could all breathe for a moment.

Who is Management?

It was the obvious question, but we didn't have an answer. They were obviously a group, a tight group that kept in close contact with one another. They had some sort of ties in with Salem's men...or perhaps Salem's men were watching them closely. There weren't any messages tying them to Salem directly.

So, who were they, and why were they so important?

This would be a perfect time for R to show up with some "deus ex machina" advice.

I leaned on the desk, nearly knocking over a vase that held oddly colored tulips. A message sent from Management 4 to 5, then from 4 to 1, following one from 5 to 3, and then 2 to 5. I rubbed my chin and stared closely at the holograms. If we don't know who or what, maybe we can figure out the...where.

"Faylin, can you figure out where these messages were sent from?" That could give us something, if anything.

"I can attempt to, Mr. Scarlet." Faylin began typing away on the keyboard's hologram, bringing up a series of numbers on a new set of screens.

"54...0...37...14...What's with all these numbers?" Each message sender and recipient had a pair of numbers for each message, making for at least a page of numbers.

My head spun just looking at them all. It didn't seem like any type of coding? It wasn't any type of code that I knew, nor was it any type of binary.

"Well, they don't seem random...there's a pattern somewhere." Casteri and Faylin stared harder at the numbers.

"I will download these to an info-chip; it might be useful later o-"

"Latitude's!"

Faylin paused the download as Lanker jumped in. "Dudes, those are latitudes and longitudes. I'd recognize them anywhere."

"Latitude and longitude, are you sure?" Faylin resumed the download while Lanker scrutinized the screen. He jabbed the hologram with a finger.

"I'm sure. The coordinates of the message from Management 5 begin with 54 and 0, right? That's the Northern region, around the capital."

I chuckled; Lanker would never cease to amaze me.

I grabbed the papers on the table and shoved them in my coat. "I like it, it's a good lead, let's grab what we can and head out of here."

The others looked slightly confused. "Leave?" Tyrinie questioned. "I thought we were going to destroy this place?"

R had told me to listen to my instincts, and something was telling me that this "Management" had more of a role than I thought. I didn't think the powerhouses themselves were a problem anymore.

"No, we're going to leave this place. We got what we came for." I motioned the team out of the ransacked office.

"What did we get?" Lanker asked in a hushed whisper as we rounded the corner.

"Information. Information we are going to stay up all night and analyze." I chuckled as the rest of the team groaned to the idea.

I took one last look around the office and followed my crew out.

END OF CHAPTER 1

2

AN OLD FRIEND

After another twenty minutes or so of walking down the dark corridors, we ended up in a separate wing of the powerhouse. A completely different way than how we came in. This area looked like the hangar in Tyrinie's home. It was so large and open that the ceiling could barely be seen.

We walked across the metal grated walkway in the upper part of the hangar, completely invisible to the guards far below us.

"Captain!" Lanker hissed suddenly, freezing in place.

I jumped, gripping the wall behind me to keep my balance. The walkway was fairly narrow without Lanker startling me.

"What Lanker?"

When there wasn't a response, I looked back and saw Lanker crouched down, looking at the group of guards below. He looked back at me and pointed frantically.

What was he pointing at?

I looked even closer when I saw a head of curly blonde hair suddenly in view.

Wait a moment...was that- "Senna? What's he doing here?"

Senna, along with about ten other men was chained by their wrists, and being led onto a large bus.

"Where are they taking him?" Lanker clenched onto the walkway and leaned in further. "Mierda! I can't hear what they are saying."

There were over two dozen guards and by the way most of them were slouching, I assumed they were humans.

Most were standing side by side holding weapons and watching their prisoners loading the bus.

Did they raid the compound Senna was at? Why were they taking him? All of the other prisoners looked rather young as well.

"Come on everyone, we need to keep moving."

"But what about Senna?" Lanker asked, wide-eyed.

"This walkway goes down a bit lower up front. We can find where they are going from there." I gave Lanker a reassuring smile as we kept moving. "Don't worry, we'll get him."

Despite the fact Senna was next to no help, he obviously meant something to Lanker, even though he would deny that.

The path was slick since the walkway ended and we were forced to move to the pipes that were lining the wall. While the view was lovely, the actual act proved to be a tad difficult. Thankfully the others didn't seem to have too much of a problem balancing. Especially Tyrinie, who seemed to slide across the pipes without any sort of trouble...must be the cat genes.

The walls began trembling as the bus below veered to life, trudging over the slick floor and out of the hatch. Most of the guards boarded the ship, leaving about a dozen left.

"They're leaving!" Lanker tried and failed to keep his composure as he watched his step bother being driven away.

"Don't worry, Lanker." The walk down would take too long, but there were more wires and pipes along the wall leading down to the ground floor. "They won't be gone for long." I turned ahead and grabbed onto one of the wire, giving it a test pull.

"Mr. Scarlet, what are you doing?"

I hopped off the pipe and locked my legs together. "Finding a faster way down. Now let's go get our nurse!" I loosened my grip and began sliding down the thick wire at breakneck speed.

This needed to be handled with some nanoid assistance.

I saw twelve guards, and there were five of us. This would be a fun fight.

My feet hit the ground with a thump as I quickly pulled out my red-hued sword, surveying the scene and waiting for the rest of the team.

I didn't have to wait for long.

"Tyrinie and Casteri, you take the group at the door. Lanker and Fay get the four at the docking line. I'll take the ones in the center. Let's go!"

We broke into our groups and charged forward, weapons at the ready. The guards noticed us, and reached for their weapons as well, pulling out sharp and polished swords.

"You children are trespassing on government property drop your weapons at once!" The man ahead of me parried my blow.

"Yea, tell me something I don't know." I grinned, pushing forward and swinging my foot at his ankles. It's a good thing Fay had been helping me train, a hit from this guy didn't hurt half as much as a solid punch from a humanoid.

I stepped on the guy that was down, holding him in place as I swung at the other man, only getting a good shot across his arm. I froze momentarily, holding back the urge to use my powers.

There were too many people here to do that. Instead, I allowed the red mist to flood into my sword, making the code-like markings glow.

The alarm went off in the hangar, flooding the room in a blinding red light. In a few minutes, we would have the entire compound flooding this place.

Looks like it was time to get going.

I slashed the last two men down, stopping them from chasing us.

"Time to go team!" I seemed to be the last one to finish since all of the other guards seemed incapacitated.

The hangar was fairly empty; most of the gear was gone. But there was one piece that stuck out to me. A car...a row of cars, all with Salem's symbol on the top.

"Everybody this way" Of course all of the cars were locked, but I'm sure we could find a way to make it start.

"Over there! Halt!" At the top of the hangar stormed more troops, but these men were bigger and had larger weapons. They began marching down the staircase, storming in our direction.

I ran to the nearest car and bashed my elbow into the window, reached in and unlocked it.

"Everyone in! Casteri, you take the wheel." I prayed that Casteri knew how to drive because I sure didn't.

I jumped over the hood and went in the passenger side as Casteri took the wheel, Faylin and the others piled in the back seat.

Gunshots went off, scraping against the car and ground as the men got even closer. I had no idea what Casteri was doing, but he was doing something with the CHEM trying to get it to start.

"Come on...come on- got it!" The engine came to life as Casteri jump-started the CHEM. "Hold on tight everyone."

We went zero to a hundred in no time, skidding out of the hangar as the guards reached the car.

"They're trying to lock us in" Tyrinie yelled, pointing at the rapidly closing hangar entrance.

"This is going to be a tight squeeze." Casteri slammed down on the pedal, making all of our heads slam against our seats. The top of the car scraped against the door as we zoomed out seconds before it slammed shut.

For a moment none of us breathed.

"That was amazing!" I laughed, trying to calm down my beating heart. "Is everyone else okay?"

I peaked in the back seat; Tyrinie was shaking and wide-eyed, clutching onto our bag of information for dear life, Lanker looked like he was about to be sick, and Faylin looked just a bit more out of sorts than usual.

I smiled. "It wasn't perfect, but we did pretty well back there. But now it's time for a rescue."

The way we came out lead to another back entrance of the level that we were on. There was a tunnel ahead that had a blinking car icon on the top. It looked like the transit tunnel was the only way to drive back down to ground level, and that has to be where that other bus went.

"Into that tunnel Casteri, when we hit the ground, we need to get to the ship ASAP."

We started down the downward metal passageway, attempting to speed past all the cameras and blinking alarms.

"The ship? What about Senna?" Lanker leaned forward in anticipation.

"We'll get Senna, the ship will be faster, and it'll be better to be able to grab him and go instead of double backing. Trust me on this."

"Okay...I trust you, Cap."

For someone who seemed to despise his stepbrother, he sure was worried about him. I could understand loving and caring for your family, but Lanker looked like he was on the verge of a panic attack. His foot was bouncing up and down, and his fingers were drumming on the window at an even faster pace.

His forehead was sweaty and his bangs were sticking up in all different directions. Although I think everyone's adrenaline was still high thanks to that quick escape.

We reached the end of the tunnel and the bright evening sun came into view. Thankfully the storm came to an end and the wind was finally dying down.

"The ship should be about a mile to our left." Lanker cut in, still bouncing in his seat.

"Got it." Casteri hadn't said more than a few words of his own, I guess he was still a bit in shock.

"Okay team, when we get to the ship, Lanker's going to jump on the helm. Casteri and Fay will provide cover, and Tyrinie and I are going to board the bus and get Senna out of there.

"What? Why can't I help?" Lanker asked.

"I need you to trail us with the ship, you'll be our getaway. We're going to have to load onto the bus while moving, and I trust you to hold her steady enough for that to happen safely. Any questions?"

"No Captain!" Everyone responded.

The Seven Seas came into view, still as strong and beautiful as ever. It's too bad we'll have to ditch the car. Even though it did have anti-gravity capability, like everything nowadays, I couldn't exactly have a car just sitting on the deck.

"Casteri, is there possibly a place for us to keep this beauty? She could come in handy later on." This car did get us out of a pretty sticky situation.

"Well, I was working on a hangar for the crew. I used the bottom of the ship. It was empty beforehand so Faylin and I redid it."

I swear I love these guys.

"Well then load her up, we're keeping her." Casteri pulled the car up to the broadside of the ship, directly under the words "SEVEN SEAS".

"Okay, let's see if this works...I haven't exactly tested it out yet." Casteri pulled up his sleeves and activated a metal cuff that was around his wrist, making the small tubes of CHEM light up. It had all sorts of buttons on it, but the big blue one seemed to stand out the most. He pressed the largest button and waited as the ground began to rumble and a side panel on the broadside slowly fell open.

My jaw followed suit; the hangar looked amazing! I didn't realize how much extra space was at the bottom of the ship. What was down there at first anyway?

It was metal from top to bottom with pipes of CHEM and wires running throughout.

There was a large desk filled with scrap metal and what looked like some sort of huge mainframe along the side.

I guess everything that ran the Seven Seas went through there.

We drove up the ramp and parked the car in the center, right against the large metal table. Casteri shut the CHEM down and slumped into his seat as the engine went silent.

"Alright team, everyone restock your weapons then meet me on the deck."

"Aye Aye" Everyone hopped out the car and scrambled up the staircase to the weapons hall. Faylin and I lagged behind the rest, heading straight to the top.

"How are you feeling, Mr. Scarlet?" Faylin kept up with my steps, holding all the papers from the powerhouse.

"I'm fine, don't worry. We've got to hurry and get Senna though. We should be able to catch them with our ship's speed." I looked back over at him as we reached the hatch to the deck. "Do me a favor and put all the files we found in the war room."

"Yes, Captain." Faylin gave a nod as he sped off to the other room.

The sun was bright as I popped up on the deck. The helm was still locked, but I didn't have to mess with it since Lanker came bursting through the hatch moments later.

"I've got it, Cap." I moved to the side as Lanker grabbed the helm and typed in a long code, causing all of the lights to begin flickering and the ship to veer to life.

"Alright Lanker full speed...that way." I pointed slightly to the right. If I was right, that was the direction the bus should have gone in.

Lanker nodded and got the ship airborne, speeding forward and knocking me back slightly.

Tyrinie and Faylin surfaced soon afterward, bright new weapons in tow.

"Ready, Captain?" Faylin asked with his hands crossed behind his back. I nodded.

"Okay, once we are in view of the bus, Lanker is going to keep the ship steady and lower her down about halfway." Casteri popped up from the hatch and joined us. "From there, Faylin and

Casteri will enter through the doors closest to the front, while Tyrinie and I enter from the back. You both will provide cover while Tyrinie and I help Senna out and up aboard the ship. Any questions?"

"No Captain!"

I nodded with a smile. "See anything yet-"

"Bus straight ahead! Full speed!"

"Alright everyone," I yelled out, tightening my coat, "get in position!"

END OF CHAPTER 2

3

THE NURSE SHAKEDOWN

Casteri and Faylin grabbed the ropes on the near end of the ship, while Tyrinie and I grabbed the ropes on the far end. It was simple enough; grab onto the rope for dear life and use it to lower down onto a huge, moving, armed, Salem-filled bus transporting prisoners to who-knows-where.

This would be more fun than I thought!

"On my word...go!"

Gripping the rope, we each jumped off the side and began sliding at breakneck speeds down the rope. I allowed the red appendages from my palms to slip out for a moment, giving me extra grip. Everyone else seemed to be going at the same speed.

"Is this going to work Captain!?" I could barely hear Tyrinie yelling over the sound of wind rushing past me.

"There! Just aim for the back of the bus." The bus was rather narrow; we'd have to gain some swinging momentum before actually jumping. "Try to rock yourself towards the bus; you'll need to aim it perfectly!"

Tyrinie's claws dug deeper into the rope as he yelped and tried to climb back up.

"Tyrinie, you'll be fine, just trust me!"

"Trust you? Are you crazy? You're going to kill me!"

"You've trusted me this far!" I kicked my legs back and forth, aiming myself towards the bus. "I'll jump first, just watch me, okay?"

I took a deep breath and counted to three as I released my hands and tumbled onto the back of the bus with a loud thump. Laughing with the remaining amount of air in my lungs, I held out my hand. "You're next Tyrinie! I got you!" He shuddered and slid back down, nearing the edge of the rope. Copying how I rocked back and forth, he gained momentum and began wildly swinging over the bus, passing it almost every time.

"Slow down a little, Tyrinie! You don't want to miss." At this rate, the guards below must've noticed us.

"Slow down, how am I supposed to slow do-" There was a resounding snap as Tyrinie's claws ripped through the rope, flinging him across.

"Damn it!" I dove to the left and caught him by the leg, both of us nearly being knocked off. "You okay?"

His arms were trembling as he stood and brushed himself off. "Do I look fine, shit head?"

The bus began swerving erratically, attempting to knock us off. I supposed it was about time they attempted something.

Faylin and Casteri made it onto the front of the bus, two carts up, with minor difficulty and signaled that they were ready to go.

"Give'em hell guys!" I yelled, giving the "victory" sign.

Casteri used his boot to smash in the glass opening, making a way for him and Faylin to jump in. I nodded at Tyrinie, slipping down the back end of the bus.

"We'll go in through here; it'll be a perfect place to slide Senna out." We hopped aboard the metal balcony on the rear and forced open the door. This bus was much larger than it looked on the outside, from where we were, we couldn't even see Faylin and Casteri.

"Senna?" Running up the aisle did no good, I didn't see him anywhere, but there were a lot more people on board than I thought. Most of them looked scared and tired.

Oddly enough, none of them even acknowledged our presence. They were looking straight ahead, purposely not looking in our direction.

"Senna?" We kept our heads down as glass flew and shots were fired from the other half of the bus. Sadly we couldn't see anything; large doors separated sections of this bus.

"Come in, Casteri! Are you guys okay?"

There was static on the other end before Casteri's voice fizzled in.

"Taking fire Captain, as to be expected." He paused for a moment before continuing. "Nothing we can't handle, though."

I sighed. "Stick to the plan, we'll be out in a moment!"

I nodded to Tyrinie, as I dashed up the aisle. "Senna? Senna!" Where was he?

We hit the door leading to the next section of the bus. It wasn't locked, but with the way that everyone was so afraid to get up, I saw why it didn't have to be.

"Come on. Tyri."

"Don't call me that." He replied quickly, nearly cutting me off.

I rolled my eyes as we entered the next section. "Senna?"

"Huh?" A voice replied.

I ran up to the third row, nearly tripping along the way. "Senna! It's about time we found you." I forced a smiled. He looked the same as a few days ago, but instead of being in his nurse attire, he was wearing some weird black jumpsuit. Come to think of it, everyone on this train was wearing that same jumpsuit.

"Lanker's friend? What in Neutopia are you doing here?" Senna looked around frantically, hardly staying in his seat. "Where is that little idiot? What have you all done now?"

"Don't worry; we're here to rescue you!" I placed my hand on his shoulder, trying to calm him down. He was more frantic than Lanker was a little while ago.

"I don't think so!" He yanked his arm away from me, dropping his voice to a whisper.

"Whatever it was that y'all did caused my compound to be raided, and me to be arrested. You must be out of your mind thinking I would go anywhere with you."

"Senna, we need to get out of here, now! It's dangerous."

He kept his head forward, not listening to a word.

It was becoming harder and harder for me to keep my patience. I moved my hand from Senna's shoulder and brought it to his collar, gripping it tightly as my eyes began to glow red. I tried to force R back. "Listen to me. Lanker isn't going to forgive me if anything happens to you. So you can either walk out with me, or I can break your legs and drag you out. Your choice! But I'm not letting my crew get hurt while you ignore me." I pointed over to the door separating us from Faylin and Casteri. "Do you hear that? Those are *my* men over there holding off the guards that were holding *you* hostage. If they get hurt because you're being an ass, guess who's getting hurt next?"

Both Senna and Tyrinie's eyes widened, by the time I was done with my spiel.

"Impressive." I faintly heard Tyrinie mumble.

Before Senna could respond, another guy spoke up.

"You should listen to him, Senna. It sounds like your step-bro did a lot to get you outta here." The guy sitting next to Senna smiled and elbowed him lightly. He had dark skin, a bright smile, and a muscular build very similar to R.

Whoever he was, he got Senna to listen.

"Fine." Senna stood to his feet. "I'll go with you, but don't think this is permanent. I'm leaving as soon as we get somewhere safe."

"Yea, sure." I grabbed Senna by the arm and pulled him further out of his seat before calling into my communicator. "I have the package; Tyrinie and I are heading back up. It's time to go Fay and Casteri!"

"Aye Aye, Captain!" Casteri responded. "We are heading up now."

At least they were safe.

Before we got too far, Senna stopped and looked back. "I'm not leaving you here, Marcus. Why don't you come too? We can both get out of this hellhole."

The guy from earlier stood to his feet. He was even taller than I thought. "Are you sure? Is that cool with you, little man?"

I shivered lightly. Did he just call me "little man?" He even talks like R, and that thought was unnerving.

"Yes, sure, it's fine. We just have to get out of here."

Marcus grabbed a black bag that was above their seat before he hopped over and ran down the aisle with us. "You don't have to tell me twice, little man." He laughed.

Before we knew it, we were back on the metal ledge, the Seven Seas in all her glory trailing behind us in a deafening roar.

I yelled into the earpiece. "Captain to Lanker! Let down the ladder, we're ready for pick up."

"Gotcha Cap- ladder coming now!" The retractable ladder rolled off of the edge of the ship, fluttering wildly in the wind.

"And…gotcha!" I lunged and grabbed the end, bracing myself against the railing to anchor it down. "Okay, Senna and the new guy head up first."

Senna paused, "You guys are younger and you both should go first!"

"Yes, but I'm the Captain and the Captain goes last. So hurry and start climbing!"

Senna reluctantly grabbed onto the ladder and began climbing up through the harsh winds. I vaguely saw Faylin and Casteri waiting for us at the top.

"I held my grip as the ladder buckled under Senna's weight.
"You're next, new guy!"

"You got it, little man. The name is Marcus, by the way." He gave me a two-fingered salute before grabbing the ladder and heading up.

Senna was clear and already on board, Marcus was going pretty fast as well.

"Alright Tyrinie, you're up."

"Yea, I know." He hopped on the railing before falling into the ladder, gripping it tightly. He barely went up five or so before turning around. "Are you coming or what?" He sounded agitated as usual, but also a little bit concerned.

"I'll go once you go up about half way. I got to keep a lookout." Casteri and Faylin seemed to have knocked out the guards for the time being. But with them probably about to wake up, and this bus currently being unmanned, we needed to hurry.

Tyrinie grumbled before crawling up a bit faster, reaching the halfway point in no time.

"Alright Scarlet, time to go." I chanted before releasing my grip on the bar while tightening my grip on the ladder, allowing both of us to fly free. Thankfully, by the time the motion hit the top of the ladder; Casteri already grabbed Tyrinie's hand and hoisted him up. I held on tight and climbed up the ladder that was now flying horizontally.

I barely reached the top rung before I felt three sets of hands yank me onboard.

"Watch your step Captain." Casteri caught me as I wobbled a bit.

"I'm okay, thank you." I nodded. "Are you guys okay? You both did a great job down there."

Casteri and Faylin were both covered with a few scrapes and dirt, but they seemed good. I was worried about them, and I meant exactly what I said to Senna. If something had happened to them down there, I didn't know what I would have done.

The thought honestly scared me.

I didn't have time to reflect, because it looked like Senna and Lanker were about to go at it.

I grumbled as I walked over.

Those two better not start fighting on my ship.

Oddly enough though, they weren't saying anything. They were just glaring at each other, both sets of arms crossed and all traces of worry and panic long forgotten.

"Well isn't this beautiful, again your reckless behavior has ruined another aspect of my life." Senna grumbled, nose high and arms tightening.

"Ruined? I just saved your life! You could at least pretend to be grateful." Lanker shot back.

The rest of us stood, not really certain if we should interfere or not.

"Grateful? For what? I'm a fugitive now, I escaped custody. Just because you don't care about your future, doesn't mean I don't care about mine."

"Your future? You wouldn't have had much of a future if you stayed on that bus."

"And whose fault was that?" Senna snapped. "I swear whenever I'm around you, something bad happens!"

"Okay, both of you calm down." I walked in-between Senna and Lanker, nearly burning from both of their glares. "Senna, listen, I know you're mad and you didn't want this to happen. But it did. If it wasn't for Lanker, we wouldn't have even noticed you, let alone rescued you. You know as well as anyone else what happens to people who are taken. Your chances weren't looking too good."

"Also," Faylin chimed in from the railing. "You work in a rebel compound. There is a 78% chance Lanker was not the cause of your compound being raided. However, there is a high chance the raid happened simply due to the nature of the place you work in."

I nodded. "So, can we not argue? We have a lot more important things to handle at the moment."

The both of them were quiet, most of the tension gone. "I won't force you to join my crew Senna, but while you are on my ship you will abide by my rules. If you want us to drop you off at our next destination, we will do so. You are a bit more dangerous to us anyways with that collar still on."

Senna looked at his collar before looking at ours, realizing they were gone and replaced with our red ones. His eyes went wide again before he shut his mouth and simply walked away.

I shook my head.

It was times like these I was glad to not have siblings.

END OF CHAPTER 5

THE COMPUTER WIZ

During the entire fiasco, Marcus has barely said a word. I really didn't know much more about him, besides his name.

Was he a friend of Senna?

"Marcus?" Rather than just reading him, I tried a different approach.

I walked over to the railing he was standing by. He was looking over the edge with an odd curiosity. But I guess it wasn't every day you got rescued by a gang of rebels.

"Oh! Hey there, little man. Thanks for getting me out of that situation. That could have been much trickier on my own." He held out his hand with a bright smile. "I don't believe I officially introduced myself. The name's Marcus, Marcus Stokes."

I returned the handshake. "I'm Captain Scarlet of the Seven Seas Faction of the Rebel Guild. It's a pleasure to meet you."

His hand was twice the size of mine.

I chuckled, "So, are you friends with Senna?"

I looked over at Lanker, who was still pouting at the helm as Casteri attempted to cheer him up.

"No, I don't know Senna. We actually just met at the holding cell." He responded. "We were all taken from different places; I was actually grabbed in the sector adjacent to Senna's. But after we were all taken, we were placed in some weird cell room. Since we were both around the same age, I naturally went over and tried to make a friend." Marcus paused as he laughed. "He was a bit harder to crack than I thought."

I didn't know how Marcus was able to crack into Senna, because we sure as hell weren't able to. The thought of Senna being friends with someone as nice as Marcus was a bit mind-boggling.

"Well, maybe you'll be able to calm him down." I laughed as I signaled Marcus to follow me. "So, what were you doing aboard that bus anyway?"

Marcus didn't seem like the kind of guy to seek out trouble.

"Well, let's just say I might have done something I wasn't exactly supposed to do." He laughed and linked his hands above his head. "It was nothing illegal, per se."

"Hmm, well where are you from?" I asked as I flagged over Casteri and Faylin.

"I'm from the Northern region, Sector 7, the capital city."

The Northern region? He sure is far from home.

"Wow, impressive." I chuckled as the others came over. "Sorry for having to cut our conversation short, but I'm going to have to take care of some business. Feel free to make yourself comfortable."

I still had all of the information from that powerhouse to go through: those coordinates, the messages, and the "Management". It all had to be connected to the other powerhouses, and in turn, connected to Salem.

I wasn't about to let this lead slip from my fingers.

"Casteri, could you start sifting through those files? I know that some of them are locked, but could you and Faylin do some digging?"

Casteri nodded, "Aye Aye, Captain."

"Maybe I could be of assistance?" Marcus walked back to where we were. "I know I'm not a member of your crew, but this is the kind of stuff that I do!"

"Really?" He seemed trustworthy enough. Honestly, I didn't even feel the need to read him.

"You mentioned locked files, yea? That's my specialty. I'm a tech specialist."

"You would help us? Just like that?" There's nice, and then there's unusually nice. Using your specialty to help a group of wanted strangers falls into the category of unusually nice.

"You did rescue me. Would it put you at ease if I said that this could be some sort of…payment for your help?" He shrugged, smiling the whole time.

"Okay, if you insist. Follow us." We headed down the hatch; me in front, and the others lagging behind. I already heard Casteri and Marcus striking up a conversation.

We entered the War Room in all of its glory. The table still had the hologram of Neutopia up, along with the new files we discovered. All of the various files were clustered in cyberspace, connected by streams of binary code. I felt a tug as something tried to pull me closer, but I pushed back.

"Well, this is what we have." I walked over and grabbed the hologram of one of the files that I recognized. It was a letter being sent from Management 4 to Management 1. "We know of an organization called The Management, and we know they have some connection to Salem." I held off the information about the powerhouses. I didn't want to risk anything by telling him everything.

Marcus paused and dropped the bag he was holding, all traces of humor falling off his face. "Whoa, Senna wasn't lying when he said that you guys were planning on taking out Lord Salem."

"Wait, he said that?" No wonder he got himself arrested! Then he blamed us for that?

"Yea, hang on a second." Marcus tied his dreadlocks back and began digging in his bag, pulling out a pair of gloves. These were weird though; they were jet black with some sort of yellow glowing CHEM pattern flowing through. I didn't even know CHEM came in yellow. "This is interesting, seems like we are on the same page here, little man."

I stood behind him to get a better look as he reached into one of the locked files, prompting a couple of red coded error screens to pop up.

That didn't look good. "Uh oh, is something wrong?"

He chuckled, lining up all of the error screens in a row. "Not at all, these guys just don't want to come out and play. Do me a favor, Captain little man, hand me the black square in my bag."

I reached over in the bag and felt around. There were clothes; both Senna's and what I assumed belonged to Marcus, along with a tiny box that was no bigger than my hand.

"Is this it?" I questioned as I placed it on the table.

"Yup, now, press the top."

I pushed the top, making it sink about an inch before the entire lid started to pulse and shake. "Whoa! Did I break it?"

"Nah, it's cool, little man. Now, peel it apart and pull out the metal thing inside."

I did as he said and pulled out a little black bar. It looked a bit like the info chip that Lanker found.

"Great, now plug that into the metal panel." Marcus nodded in the direction of the panel. Once inserted, another surge seemed to flow through the room, making my entire body go numb.

"Now we're cooking!" Marcus dropped his hold of the multiple error screens as three black and yellow hologram keyboards appeared in front of him.

"Wait a moment, I've seen those before." Casteri walked over to Marcus' side as he began typing away on all three boards, flooding the entire screen in code. "Where did you get access to that? That's not ordinary tech gear."

It did look a bit advanced, but what did I know…I was from the West.

To my surprise, Marcus just laughed. "Okay, you might be a little bit right. I'm not exactly just a tech specialist. But we can talk about that later on."

"What are you then, really? And where did you learn how to do that?" Casteri was right, Marcus was impressive. He already unlocked three of the locked files, and he was barely looking at the screen. His hands were flying and nothing but code was literally bouncing off the walls.

"I'm a holographic database analyzer"

A what?

"You're a hacker." Casteri replied as more of a statement than a question.

"Nah, holographic database analyzer sounds much cooler." Marcus laughed, continuing his work.

"I'm sorry, what? What does that mean?" I really didn't want to sound stupid, especially since I'm in a room with a bunch of geniuses.

"Got it!" The screen beeped as all of the binary images began fading away and the normal color returned to the room. The files that were locked were now open, and even more documents began scanning through. "I can explain my job to you, little man. But, it is kind of a secret." He paused and turned to face me, still typing with his other hand. "Here's some information about our Lord Salem. You see, Lord Salem doesn't like all of his information being in physical form. So, he has a…branch of workers who have the exclusive job of keeping his cyberspace files safe. Not many people can decipher or even understand holographic binary, so the few people that can are called HD-Basers, or just Basers for short. I'm technically not a certified baser, but I was next in line to become one."

This had to have been fate,

"Wait, but if you are one of the few people that can understand all of this stuff, why were you on the run?"

"Well about that." The typing stopped as all of the open documents in the locked file popped up, revealing more notes, articles, and census information. "I might have hacked into some…restricted information." Marcus laughed.

Names of people that were marked as rebels, and people who were "terminated" popped up, along with a few scattered names listed under Management. "Something about Salem rubbed me wrong the day I met him. Ever since then, I've been doing some digging and got myself black-listed. I had to skip town before Salem's men came for me. There are things in cyberspace that even we aren't supposed to access."

I nodded, still focusing on all of the holograms of information that floated around the table.

"Marcus, how would you like to join the Seven Seas faction?" I outstretched my hand, wincing as it was grabbed tightly.

"I thought you'd never ask!" He laughed, shaking my hand vigorously. "I'd be honored."

I nodded. "Welcome to the crew." I paused as I began to feel dizzy, swaying a bit on my feet. "Faylin, could you show Marcus around?"

I stiffly walked out of the room before he responded, holding onto the wall for support.

This felt like what happened last time when I was in my office, and I found myself in that strange red world.

I couldn't see straight, and the hallway seemed to stretch and skew the more I walked.

I stood still, trying to calm the nausea that was making my stomach churn. My head was pounding like something was trying to pop out of my brain.

BOOM!

I jumped and grabbed my head as the noise resounded through my ears, like as explosion in my eardrums.

Then all of the sudden…there was nothing.

Everything started fading red, almost like my eyes were flooding with blood. I couldn't see, but I could feel something wet pooling and running down my face.

"Damn it…" I couldn't see a thing! I had to bite my tongue to stop myself from calling out for help.

"I'm scared."

I was scared; Father wasn't around to solve it his time, and it felt so much worse than before.

Where was I? Where did I wander off to? This has never happened before.

"Oof!" I tripped down a flight of stairs, landing face first onto the floor. I felt around, but I couldn't tell. I know I could figure it out if I focused, but nothing was making sense.

"C'mon, breathe…" Where was R, why wasn't he helping me? I just sat and laid my head against the wall. Hopefully, this would just…wear off. I touched my face, it was wet, but I couldn't tell what was making it that way. I know I wasn't crying, and I prayed I wasn't bleeding, but the more I moved my eyes around, the more it hurt.

The red started fading to black, and my head became heavier and heavier.

Huh…

I opened my eyes, only to be greeted by red hazy mountains. This was the same place from last time. I looked down; my outfit was the same that it was last time that I came…here. But, where is here exactly?

"Hello?"

I moved my foot, and surprisingly, I could walk. Last time I felt glued to the floor, but now, despite my legs feeling heavy, they worked fine. I looked around, turning in complete circles. The sky was so dark that it nearly looked black, and every few moments, streams of jagged lightning would stream against the sky.

This place seemed completely barren and lifeless. "Hello? Is anyone here?"

I began walking towards one of the valleys directly between two of the largest mountains. As I got closer, I began to see lights.

I sprinted forward, nearly reaching the edge of the cliff before pausing in complete awe.

There was an entire civilization. It looked similar to one of the sky cities, but far more advanced.

The buildings all looked like holograms, but with mass. Different items seemed to fizzle in and out of existence, disappearing and reappearing in different locations. And the "people"…were flying? All of them were jumping and gliding from place to place.

I must be hallucinating.

"Welcome home." A voice spoke behind me, startling me as my arms were grabbed.

Before I could turn, my limbs froze again, and everything went blurry before fading to black.

The light was too bright; it sent shocks right to my head. My eyes itched and all I wanted to do is scratch them.

I raised the back of my hand to my left eye, preparing to rub it fiercely.

"Stop! Don't do that!" A voice shouted out.

I paused and my hand jerked away. Who was that? Where was I? The Med Bay? Why was I here?

Oh, right. I passed out…in the hallway I think. All of the memories came back; everything turning red, my eyes leaking thick liquid-stuff, that pulsing headache and booming noise. What the hell was all of that?

I tried to sit myself up before I was stopped again. "Will you just sit still?"

The voice came closer, and all I saw was a familiar mop of curly blonde hair.

Senna?

"Senna? What are you doing here? What am I doing here?"

He sighed, placing his clipboard on the sterile white table before coming over to my bedside. "Do you remember anything?"

Was this the "nurse" in him, he seemed a lot nicer than usual.

"No, I mean, yes, but, nothing that makes sense. Were my...eyes bleeding?"

He came closer and placed a hand on my stomach and another one on my back. "I'm going to help you sit up, okay? Nice and easy." I squirmed and tried to relax as Senna pushed me up into a sitting position. The headache was gone, thank goodness, but the nausea persisted.

"How do you feel?" He asked, patting me lightly.

I looked around the Med Bay, it looked nice in here, like a real hospital. There was even one of those needle drippy-things in my arm. I'd seen them on TV time and time again.

Moving my eyes around didn't hurt as much as it did before, but they still felt a bit sore and sluggish, almost like I was opening my eyes underwater.

"I feel...alright."

"Good." Senna smiled, adjusting his nurse tunic. "You gave us quite the scare."

"Us?" I questioned, eyeing the basin of water and bloody rags next to the bed.

"Yes." He caught my glance and hurried over to move the basin. "Your humanoid, Faylin, found you and brought you in here. I was already here and I insisted that I watch over you."

"You didn't have to; Faylin has taken care of me before."

"Yes, but a humanoid isn't a doctor, is it?" There was a lot more spite in that sentence than there needed to be.

Senna smiled and walked back to the counter, retrieving a vial of clear liquid and a cloth, before heading back to me.

"This might sting just a bit, but we'll need to clean this up." He took a seat in the chair by my bedside and dumped the foul-smelling liquid on the cloth.

To my surprise, before he even put it on my face, he grabbed my hand and gave it a squeeze of reassurance. "It won't hurt for long, okay?"

Who was this person?

"You have…quite the strange body, don't you?" Senna asked as he wiped the area around the corner of my eyes.

You have no idea.

"I guess. This happens every once in a while, so there is no need to panic." I responded, enjoying the pampering. My parents were never this gentle whenever my genetics decided to backfire on me.

Was this how it's supposed to feel?

I was jarred from my thoughts when Senna's hand froze in place. "Once in a while?"

"Yes…" I said, hesitantly. "But…it's not like it's a big deal. Just a little fainting spell."

Father explained this to me long ago.

I'm one of the first of my kind, a prototype, and one of the only two people in existence to have a nanoid infused within me. There are always…things wrong with the prototype. Once I complete my mission, they might have time to fix me up and perfect me.

So my body backfiring is nothing out of the ordinary.

Sometimes I would drop for no reason. I could be out for minutes, or even days. Nobody would truly know. While these set of symptoms were new, the concept wasn't.

"No!" He gasped before catching himself, "This is not simply a fainting spell. An episode like that one time is bad enough, but this has been happening multiple times. Why the hell didn't your parents send you to a hospital in the North sooner?"

Only people who were on death's door were shipped to the North for emergency care. I rolled my eyes.

"Listen, we need to run some tests and I'll do what I can--"

Captain, you are needed in the Parley Hall, Captain to Parley Hall. Thank you!

Was that an intercom? When did we get a VI intercom? Why does everyone change things when I'm sleeping?

That is pretty cool, though.

"Looks like the team needs me, thanks for taking care of me, Senna." I pulled my hand from his and wiped some of the excess liquid from my face.

"Wait, you're not well yet! You just woke up." Senna grabbed his clipboard and shot up after me.

"That reminds me, how long was I out?"

"Out? Three days, you were unconscious for three days!"

I paused, three days? I shook my head; I'd worry about that later. Seeing how much I had missed was the top priority.

"Well, at least let me bandage you up, please. Your arm is bleeding."

I looked down before hitting the door. My injection site was puffy and swollen, and sure enough, it was bleeding.

It must have been from me pulling out the needle drippy-thing. I smiled and wiped the blood off, smearing it down my arm.

"It's not a big deal, thanks anyway."

I left before he could say anything else.

END OF CHAPTER 4

5

ESPIONAGE

Parley Hall wasn't too far from the Med Bay; just through the door that led to the crew's area of the ship and down the staircase next to my quarters. I must have been at this part of the ship when I collapsed; there were still a few red smears along the walls.

The whole situation was…unnerving at the least. Bleeding from the eyes? Since when was that a part of my symptoms? First vomiting blood, and now this. I didn't want to face it, but the truth was pretty apparent.

Finding out the truth about Salem, The Management and whatever the hell else was going on might be the least of my concerns.

Because I might not live long enough to make it happen.

Before, Father told me there was little that could kill me in this world, the nanoids will fix themselves at rapid rates and do whatever they can to keep and preserve me, their vessel. But, if my body decided to turn on me and reject itself – there's little that R could do to save me.

"Okay, enough of that talk." I took a deep breath and puffed out my chest, trying to seem as calm as possible as I entered the Hall. All I had to focus on was killing Salem before this thing inside of me had a chance to kill me first.

The team seemed nice and relaxed, oddly enough. Marcus, the newest member, was seated on top of one of the tables with Casteri on his left. They seemed engaged in some sort of gadget that Casteri, no doubt, built himself.

Lanker had a map spread out over the table and seemed to be attempting to teach Tyrinie something he had no interest in. As usual, Tyrinie was perched in his seat, prim and proper, and was rolling his eyes and huffing at every word Lanker said. Faylin came in from another door with papers in his hand and joined Marcus by his side, showing him the stack and pointing out a few parts. They really all seemed like a team, and they seemed happy here.

This was good.

I smiled and cleared my throat. "Good morning, team. Have I missed much?" I joked, laughing as they all jumped at my sudden presence.

Choruses of "Good morning, Captain" and "Hello, Captain" filled the air as I walked closer.

"I am surprised you are awake and moving so quickly, we were expecting you to be asleep for much longer." Faylin questioned, setting down the papers.

"No need to worry about that. What have I missed?" I popped over to Faylin who seemed more than a little hesitant to share the papers he had in his hand with me. From what I could see, it looked like letters, more messages being sent back and forth between the Management. On the next page, there were actual names next to a certain Management number, only two were listed though.

Management 2 – Lelani Waves

Management 5 – Myrah Flynn

Myrah and Lelani? I've never heard those names before. If they were important to Salem, I thought I would have known those names.

Faylin sighed and spread the papers across the table, prompting Tyrinie and Lanker to stop and come over. "Actually Mr. Scarlet that is why we hoped you were awake. There is a lot that we need to tell you."

"Yea," Lanker chimed in, hopping on the opposite bench. "The new genius guy made this a lot easier!"

Marcus laughed, waving him off. "Come on Lanks, it wasn't just me. Faylin and Casteri were a huge help. I couldn't have done anything without them."

Lanker leaned over in my direction, whispering. "It's like they're the genius trio or something?"

With all the papers laid out, I saw exactly what they were working on while I was out. I guess they were rather busy. All of the coordinates we found in the Western powerhouse seemed to have been marked on an updated map, along with more names and the listed Management member.

"Well." Faylin started, pointing out information on the sheets. "It looks like our hunch was correct. There is definitely a connection between Salem and The Management. From what we could find using Marcus and a few of his sources, they seem to be his officers. Something like an inner circle, at least that is the conclusion we came to. Each member is stationed at a different part of Neutopia, and they each have a specific job. I believe Marcus had more information about the identities and locations of the few members we were able to identify."

Faylin nodded to Marcus who promptly stood to his feet and slapped Fay on the back. "Thanks for the intro, Fifi." With the look Faylin gave Marcus, it seemed like that nickname had been some sort of battle between the two of them. "We have five members of the illusive Management, but we only know a bit about a few of them. I've seen about two or three of them, but only in passing really. Thanks to my…job, I came in close contact with a few members of The Management. The first one is who we are currently closest to; Lelani Waves, Management number 2 and the lovely controller of the Southern powerhouse. On record, it looks like Ms. Waves is twenty-one years of age and is the heiress to the Waves family fortune."

"Why is an heiress working for Salem?" She's young, wealthy, and comes from a Southern family? There is no reason for her to have to lift her finger for anything, so why work for Salem? Marcus shrugged, sifting through his files again. "I don't know, but that is where things get weird. Half of her census information is missing."

He pulled a hologram of her census data, and sure enough, half of the information was barred out. Namely her date of birth, residence, and picture. However, in bold numbers, it did say she was twenty-one.

"According to Tyrinie, Lelani is a bit…out of time."

Tyrinie pointed to the empty date-of-birth slot. "There is no way she could be twenty-one. My family invited her over to our estate for business, and she introduced herself as being twenty-one then."

"So?" I didn't know where he was going with this.

"We invited her over nearly eleven years ago. This information is clearly wrong." Tyrinie sat back, crossing his arms.

"Can the census be wrong, Lanker?" I questioned. Lanker shook his head, placing his drink down for a moment.

"Nope, Cap. The census is updated and backed up every sixty seconds. My ma told me how the whole thing worked. It's literally impossible to hack the census."

"He's right though," Marcus chimed in again. "I've met Lelani, not personally, but I have seen her monitoring around baser headquarters up in the North. I remember seeing her years ago, and she literally hasn't changed."

A woman who doesn't age? That's impossible.

"Well, we'll have to worry about that when we meet her." I shook my head and chuckled. "It doesn't matter how old she is or

whether or not she tampered with the census. If she's associated with Salem, we already know what we have to do, right?"
It was quiet for a moment before everyone nodded. I smiled.
"Good, now where is she? Do we know where her powerhouse is?"
"Well, that's the other problem." Marcus, sliding on his black and yellow gloves, pulled up a smaller version of the hologram of Neutopia. The hologram was able to come from the glove itself.
"We don't exactly know where she is. We know it's in the capital city of the South, but that's about it. She has no other cyber trail and barely any messages in or out."
Well, that's a problem. It seemed like with every piece of good news, there's an additional piece of bad news, and it was making my head spin. Looks like I'd have to pull R in for some help with all of this.
"Okay, so in plain talk, what do we know about each member?" I rested my hand on my fist, leaning forward as Casteri took point next.
"I believe I can assist here, I've compiled a list of each member." He pushed up glasses I've never seen him wear before as he read the list.
"Management 1 – all we have is the pseudonym, Dr. C. Not much is known except for the fact he is male and works in the Eastern region powerhouse. Management 2 – Lelani Waves, heiress to the Waves family fortune and controller of the Southern powerhouse as well as the…pig farm."
"What the hell is a pig farm?" Tyrinie questioned before I had the chance.
"That I'm not sure of, but it looks like in the very few messages that Lelani sends they all seem connected to something called the *pig farm*." Casteri reshuffled his papers before beginning again.
"Continuing, we have Management 3 – no name or information found for this one either. All we know is they are in control of the

powerhouse in, none other than, Sector 6." A member of The Management in Sector 6?

That sounded like a complete nightmare. Why did Salem need one of his officers in the *most* lawless place in Neutopia?

"Are we sure they are in Sector 6? Why would Salem need anyone there?"

Marcus flipped the hologram around, showing the barren depths on the opposite side of our regions. "Well, the signal is coming from a landmass out in the middle of the ocean on the other side of the world. And it's just west of The Valley. It has to be Sector 6, no doubt."

I remembered hearing about The Valley. The infamous spot where Salem detonated the war-ending bombs nearing the conclusion of the Century War. Whatever was in them was powerful enough to wipe out life for hundreds of thousands of miles, and tear chunks of the planet right from the surface. Now, what remains is a seemingly infinitely long and deep valley that cuts through the planet like a bad scar.

"The remaining two are Management 4 and 5. We know nothing about 4, except for the fact they are in control of the Western powerhouse we already went into. Last but not least, Management 5, Myrah Flynn, is in control of the Northern region powerhouse."

Marcus began to laugh. "I know her as well. Myrah Flynn is the lead of the special tactics unit in the Northern military base. All executions driven from conspiracy-based crimes are led by her." He paused before shivering slightly. "She's like Lord Salem's personal assassin. I've seen her work, she's brutal."

"She might be brutal, but so are we." I smiled and stood up, eyeing each of my guys. "Everyone did an amazing job. We have our targets, now comes the easy part. We find them, destroy their bases, and take them out. Once his officers are gone, Salem will be nearly defenseless, and that is when we will strike."

We were another step closer, and victory was so close I could nearly taste it.

The ship was silent after the crew was sent off to bed. I almost forgot that even though I spent three days sleeping, everybody else has been staring at holograms and data. They all deserved a good night sleep at the very least.

It wasn't as if I was nervous or anxious, but realistically, I was about to *kill* someone. Actually kill someone. On this journey, my team and I would be made to kill a lot of people. A sour heaviness settled in my stomach while part of me actually *wanted* to do this. After all, for as long as I remember, I was told anyone associated with Salem deserved to die. Father told me killing was like climbing a tree; at first, it would be difficult and new and I would even make a few mistakes, but after a while, I would become a natural at it.

I could even learn to enjoy it.

"I don't know." I said to nobody. Why did I feel weird then? I sighed and lifted my left hand up to my mouth and settled the area right below my thumb beneath my teeth, biting down hard. It was a bad nervous habit I picked up years ago, but it did help to calm me down. I would just bite here and there, and when one area was too sore, I would just move to a different one. My body would basically fix the wounds within a day or so, depending on how deep it was.

I felt like something was missing. Father never mentioned anything about the Management before. I never knew Salem had officers. Why would he keep something that important away from me? I would just ask R for help, but I haven't seen him since my last blackout. He was nowhere to be found.

"Who's nowhere to be found, eh?" I jumped slightly and pulled my hand out of my mouth, shoving it under my pillow. Speak of the devil.

"Hey, R." I hoped that he didn't see anything.

"Heya kid, why so blue?" R settled down on the unoccupied part of my bed.

I laughed, head still on the pillow, facing the opposite direction. "I'm not upset, just…thinking."

"Yea, there's no point in lying to me kid. I live in your head, remember?" I could practically hear him rolling his eyes. "You're worried because things are getting pretty real now? Here you are, on your own, on a mission you weren't prepared for without daddy dearest. Plus, you've never actually killed someone before, have you?" He laughed and vanished, appearing right in front of me.

"R! Could you not do that?" I grabbed my pounding heart and slid back from his glowing, slit red eyes.

He smirked, "I'm going to help you out kiddo, and give you a much-needed confidence booster!"

I settled, dropping my hand from my nightshirt. "Really?"

"Yup, and here it is. You, my favorite and only vessel, are going to win?"

I paused, "Win against Lelani?"

He smiled again, shaking his head. "Don't think so small, you are going to win completely! You are going to beat Salem before this time next year."

My heart leapt up in my throat. "What! Really?"

Before this time next year, I would have done it, I would have beaten Salem! That also meant that I would find Father! My mission would be complete; everything I had trained and prepared for was right around the corner. If I do beat him that meant that I wasn't going to die anytime soon! This was amazing, it was-

"But… "

I paused my mental rant. "But, what?"

"…"

"R?"

"..."

"R!"

R paused for a moment, seemingly lost in thought. He glanced around the room as if he was searching for the right thing to say. "...sorry kiddo, there are...rules I have to follow. I'm not allowed to tell you everything; I don't exactly know everything yet. There are still some elements that I have to factor in. Trust me, the more I tell you, the more I risk jacking up fate, and that would only hurt you and me in the end." He shrugged.

"Unfortunately that's all I can do for you right now. Rely on *your* instincts and *your* findings. This will not go the way you think it will, but...you will accomplish your goal."

"I'm glad to hear that, I really am. But, how was this supposed to help-?" I shouted at the empty space.

Of course, he was gone.

And I was left even more confused.

END OF CHAPTER 5

THE WOMAN OF MANY FACES

"Okay, now hop up on the scale platform."

I sighed, doing what Nurse Senna said. He literally trapped me in my room and refused to let me go until I let him do an examination. I, of course, objected. But I guess I underestimated Senna's strength and the fact that he was a good half-a-foot taller than me. When I refused to budge, he simply tossed me over his shoulder and carried me to the Med Bay. Any way of escaping would've exposed me, and Senna would not have let that go. It seemed like playing along was the lesser of two evils.

Despite how mortifying it was…

Thankfully, the remainder of the crew was still asleep.

He tapped his pen on his chin as he wrote down my measurements. "You're 5'6 and barely 120 pounds?" He looked me over again as I stepped down. "I noticed that you were small for a young man your age, but I didn't realize *how* small."

"Hey, I'm not small, I'm…average." I had a decent amount of muscle for someone my age, especially from all the training I did. However, I was nowhere near the size of my father, Casteri, or Marcus.

"Trust me, nothing about you is *average*." He muttered, rolling his eyes. "You are rather small, though. When you had your black-outs, were you hooked up to an IV, or anything similar? Did you have weekly medical checks?"

I laughed, tossing a ball of gauze back and forth. "I didn't grow up in the North like you Senna; we don't have weekly medical checks or fluid-drippy things in the West."

"IV's. They are called IV's, not fluid-drippy things." He sighed again and pointed me in the direction of the bed. "Go ahead and take a seat."

I gritted my teeth and hopped over, taking a seat as Senna went in the opposite direction, grabbing some tools from the other table.

"Tell me about your life at home, Scarlet." He paused, "And do I have to keep calling you that? I know it can't be your real name, and it's a rather odd nickname."

Well, he was sort of right.

According to the documents that Discordia had on me and my existence, my name is R-001. "Scarlet" was a human name that was given to me, but I never knew who actually named me. I only assumed whoever named me chose the name "Scarlet" because of my hair. Clever!

I laughed, "It is my name believe it or not. If you don't like Scarlet, you can just call me Captain. That works too." I laid back and focused on counting the bolts in the ceiling as Senna bandaged up the bite marks on my hands. Of course he noticed, but he didn't say anything, and for that I was grateful. It was a weird thing to try to explain.

Oddly enough, the marks were still there and rather bruised. While my teeth were sharper than the average human's, scars typically didn't stay on me for very long, unless there is some sort of nerve damage. I must have bit harder than I thought.

"So, home life, remember? Start talking." He mumbled, sanitizing each indent.

Now, what the hell was I supposed to say? Going back as far as I can remember, I was trained day in and day out. Not like it ever did much good, as my body and my powers were constantly mutating and changing. I could train for weeks on one skill, and it would be completely different the next day.

I wasn't taught how to interact with humans, in fact, father tried to keep me as far away from them as possible. My training was brutal, but the punishments for failure were even worse, especially when I would be placed back in my isolation tank in the lab. By age eight, father finally realized that mother was a scheming bitch. She escaped before he could let me loose on her. But when mother left, so did what remained of father's...humanity.

If that's what you would call it.

Training became harsher, and the punishments came far more often than the praises. It was what I needed to make me who I was today.

I didn't like it, but it was necessary.

Some of the happiest times I had were the moments I could slip away and be with Persephone and Emme. I guess Senna, as a human, would see my life as being one that was pretty rough. But I didn't need a good life; I was my father's weapon, not a normal human.

A comfortable and familiar numbness filled my chest as I remembered my father's favorite statement.

"Remember R-001, I created you for the sole purpose of finishing my work, being my weapon. Your job, your only purpose in this world, is to kill Salem and anyone who defends him."

Nothing else mattered. That was my one and only purpose. The thought of it actually gave me comfort.

I paused my mental rant and tried to think of something that sounded ordinary. "Um, it was good. My mother was a good woman, a bit intense, but good. She always tried to teach me how to be just like her. But, I ...uh, I didn't always make the mark." I laughed, wincing a bit as Senna cleaned deeper around the broken skin. The medication stung. "Father was strict, and trained me to be the best." I paused, thinking of how to reword that. "I mean, he always told me to do my best. He's my hero, an absolutely perfect man."

"Okay, sit up." Senna placed his hands on my lap and back again and helped me up like last time. He pulled out a tiny looking flashlight and began to look in my ears and around my face, focusing on the marking I had underneath my eye. "Your eyes are such an odd color. I don't think I've ever seen anybody with the same shade of red." He peered even closer, making me lean back. "So, you were close to your mom?"

"No."

I spat the word out on instinct.

"Your dad, then?" Senna questioned as he shined the light in my right eye.

"My father is great, but I wouldn't say that we were close. Don't get me wrong, I love… my parents very much."

I didn't know what else to say, so I just stayed quiet.

"Well all families are different, that's understandable. Who were you close to then?" Senna shined the light in my left eye, making me see spots.

"Well, there is my neighbor, Mrs. P and her daughter, Emme. They were-"

"*Merde*!" Senna suddenly jumped back, dropping the light and running behind the next table, making me jump as well.

"Holy shit! What's the matter?"

Senna was shaking like he saw a ghost or something, still holding onto the table for dear life.

"Uh…Senna?" I said slowly, sliding off of the bed.

"No, no, no! Sit still, stay there." He released his death grip and grabbed the light that rolled under the sink. "Just sit there for a moment."

"Senna, you're kind of freaking me out. What's with you?" Did he see something? I don't do well with surprises, and seeing the normally collected Senna acting like this was too weird for comfort.

"Something moved." He stood up straight now, eyeing me wearily.

"Of course things are moving, we're on an airship-"

"In your eye, not on the ship!" He paused and took a deep breath, composing himself. "Something just moved through your iris."

"My…iris?"

"The red part of your eye, the colored part that's outside the pupil!" Senna reached for the intercom before taking another deep breath. "Marcus, would you please come to the Med Bay." Oh shit. This isn't good. I blew some of the hair out of my face and took a seat, watching as Senna paced the floor. There had to be some way I could slide out of this one.

Bits of code and blood were constantly swimming through my eyes. It was only noticeable if you stared long enough. I should have never let Senna get that close. It completely slipped my mind.

The door slid open and Marcus and Faylin came in. Marcus, black collar removed and red collar instated, had his uniform already on; black slacks, black boots, and dark gold top. The only difference was he had the jacket tied tightly around his waist, and his black and yellow gloves on and activated.

He must have already been awake and doing some work. Faylin never seemed to sleep, so the fact he was already up and in uniform was no surprise.

"You called, Sen?" Marcus waltzed over, hands linked behind his head as usual.

"Yes, I did. I-hello Faylin, I don't remember calling you." Senna replied, spite dripping in every word. I wonder what in Neutopia Faylin did to get on Senna's bad side.

Faylin, as usual, didn't seem fazed. "Marcus invited me up; we were working together on gathering more information about the

Management. When you called for him, he suggested that I come along."

Senna shot a disgruntled look at Marcus before sighing and flagging the two over to me. "Here, take a look."

Faylin cut off the CHEM flowing in the room, making the whole room go dark and my arms tense. All three of them came over and stared as Senna shined the light back into my left eye.

The room was silent for a moment before Marcus jumped back a bit. "Whoa, what was that?"

My head shifted a bit in discomfort from being stared at.

"How peculiar." Faylin slid his hand under my chin; keeping my head still. The three of them peered closer.

I just needed to play dumb for now. "Um… what are you guys seeing?"

"That's the thing, I have no idea. I've never seen this before." Senna paused and jotted some notes down. "Imagine your eye is a marble, and right now, *something* is swimming around inside of that marble."

I blinked, finally resting my eyelids and trying to seem nonchalant. "Listen, for the time being, can we just postpone talking about this? We have a lot more important things to do and whatever my eye is doing can wait, right? Out of sight, out of mind" I faked a laugh, placing my hand over my left eye.

Marcus blinked a few times before erupting in laughter and slapping me on the back. "You are crazy little man, nothing scares you! I like this kid, Senna."

"Marcus, please be serious! He could have a parasite; things don't just float around in people's eye sockets! If it's near his eyes, it could be in his brain or who knows where else." Senna replied in a panic, making Marcus shake his head.

"Don't freak the kid out, look, he looks pretty healthy. Why don't you just take a few blood samples and do some of those experiments you like so much. That way, you both can have some answers." Marcus patted Senna on the head. "So just calm down, Sen."

I don't know how Marcus is able to work his magic, but whatever he did, it seemed to work and Senna calmed down. Lanker should take lessons from this guy.

"Well, since the Captain seems to be in fine condition, I will take my leave then." Faylin gave a polite bow before exiting the room. Senna rolled his eyes.

"You know I don't like his kind." He muttered to Marcus, as if I couldn't hear.

"C'mon Sen, Faylin's a cool dude, give him a chance."

"Not on my life." Senna glanced at me for a moment, the same amount of worry on his face as he grabbed a needle. "I'm going to take some blood, hold still okay." He said softly, both Marcus and Senna headed back to the other table, facing away from me. Now, there was no way I could have him take a blood sample from me. That would be bad. Very bad!

I closed my eyes and quickly focused on my quarters, allowing the red halo to appear around my feet.

Thankfully, in less than a second, I felt myself dissolve into a stream of code and reappear in my room. I let out a sigh and flopped on my bed.

That was close.

"Okay you little twerp, since I know this isn't going to go anywhere, if I tell you to rest up and not run around, will you listen?" Senna questioned, tapping his foot outside my locked door.

After arguing and refusing tests for a good hour, I thought Senna finally gave up and allowed me to have some peace. But every time I swore he was finished, Senna would come back with another argument.

"Probably not." I laughed. "Remember, I have a crew to lead.

Plus, we are about to go after one of the members of the Management." The kinks in my back were finally worked out and I felt good as gold.

"The Management? What's that?" Senna questioned.

"Sorry, official crew business. You would know if you were a member." I taunted, grinning the whole time.

"Speaking of which, we are in the South now, so I assume you'll be leaving soon?"

There was a momentary pause before Senna answered. "My bags are already packed. This vacation has been amusing. But it's about time for me to get back to reality."

I smiled, shaking my head. I could see right through him.

I was hoping to have a little bit of silence, especially because I hadn't had a chance to message Mrs. P in days! But that wasn't about to happen.

Captain to the War room! Thank you.

I was starting to hate that intercom.

"It's about time you decided to join us, *Captain*." Tyrinie sat atop the main table in the War room, arms crossed and cloak donned as usual. "Never say I haven't done anything useful for you."

He hopped down and nudged Casteri, who in turn, activated the hologram of Neutopia. "I, Tyrinie J. Dukas, just found a way to find Ms. Waves."

Wow, Tyrinie actually did work? Shocker! "Really, where is she?"

"I don't know." Tyrinie answered, just as confident. Just what I was expecting.

"But," He continued. "I know someone who does. None other than Madam Ginseng, the woman that knows everything."

"Madam Ginseng? That is an…interesting lead." Faylin joined in. "I do not doubt she would know."

"Agreed, but isn't she a bit exclusive? Not just anyone can run and speak with Madam Ginseng." Casteri asked, pulling up what I assumed was her report.

"I know that, dumbass!" Tyrinie snapped. "Thankfully we, and by 'we' I mean the Captain and myself, are not just anyone. I'm pretty sure the Dukas family heir and a rebel Captain would prove to be a worthy audience for Madam Ginseng."

The others nodded in agreement. Was I the only one who has no clue who this woman was? "Okay, so who is this Ginseng lady anyways?"

All commotion stopped.

Tyrinie rolled his eyes. "Tell me you aren't serious. Do you seriously not know who *The* Madam Ginseng is?"

I paused before slowly walking over and taking a seat. "Am I supposed to know who she is?"

Faylin shook his head. "Unfortunately, I must agree with Tyrinie on this one. Madam Ginseng is a very well-known woman, especially in the Western and Southern regions." He pulled up another hologram, this one being a large and gaudy looking building with pink and blue floral decorations. "She is the owner of one of the most exclusive all-humanoid brothels in the South; The Tea Time Brothel."

I paused. "She's a-what now?"

"A *brothel* owner. You do know what a brothel is, right?" Tyrinie asked with arms crossed and an amused look playing across his face.

"Am I...supposed to know what that is?"

Again, the room fell silent.

To my confusion, Senna, turning completely red, busied himself with paperwork as everyone else erupted into fits of laughter. Everyone besides Faylin, who chose that time to start reading his book again.

"This is too good!" Tyrinie wheezed out, holding on to Lanker, who also looked like he was ready to pass out from laughter. "This guy is nearly my age, and doesn't know what a brothel is."

"Our hardcore Captain is an innocent little virgin!" Lanker cried out.

Virgin?

I know I've heard that term before. It had to do with sex or something like that, from what Persephone told me.

Father never saw the point in teaching me about strange sweaty human habits, since that was something I never needed to worry about. I honestly didn't even see the point. So, what did a brothel have to do with the sex act? Or Ginseng?

And what did it have to do with the mission?

Actually, that name did sound familiar. I know that I had heard it before. Ginseng. Mother must have mentioned her name at one point, I was sure of it.

"Okay okay, quiet both of you." I called out in my "captain" voice. They quieted down for the most part, but Tyrinie and Lanker still had tears in their eyes. "So, what does this woman have to do with our mission?"

"Madam Ginseng isn't just a Madam. She knows everything! Think of her as an oracle." Tyrinie sure seemed sure of this woman; I'd never seen him so animated before.

Faylin shook his head, pulling up another screen that showed men and women in their classy Southern Region Style entering the building. Many donned dark glasses and large hats while others simply waltzed in. All of them looked rushed, and slightly panicked.

"Theatrics aside" Faylin pointed at one of the men in the image. "Madam Ginseng works as an information broker. She sells and deals in information, which, for the right price, she would happily pass along to another."

Tyrinie jumped in again, an obvious expert on this topic. "I've seen people sell their mansions just to get a night with her. Along with her…other obvious services, many companies have been ruined by her information alone. She is as feared as she is respected. And I know she'll be able to give us the information we need."

It seemed like a good lead. If this woman is as good as everyone else seems to think, then this might just be worth a shot.

"If she's so exclusive, would she even want to speak with us?" I approached the hologram.

Each of the people inside seemed to be extraordinarily wealthy, and each seemed to have information that weighed a ton. "We don't have any business information. Would she even take interest in us?"

Tyrinie nodded with a fanged smirk. "As I mentioned, you are something quite out of the ordinary, and that is what Madam Ginseng preys on."

I nodded, straightening up. "We'll leave at dusk."

Everyone nodded and began to file out, a few hushed whispers and chuckles still emerging from the group.

END OF CHAPTER 6

7

OF LEADS AND LADIES

I tried to look my best. Hair combed, face clean, and captain's outfit set.

After all, it wasn't every day you met an infamous information-selling Madam. I was the only one though; everyone else was out of uniform and dressed in their best.

Finally, after an agonizing two hours of research, I discovered what "brothels" and "madams" were. It was weird, and it made me realize just how strange humans really were.

The sun had nearly set, and we were all in Casteri and Marcus' workshop. It seemed like those two completely redid the previously empty hangar at the bottom level of the ship. It now housed an updated engine that pumped CHEM to all corners of the ship. On one side of the room, tarps, blueprints, and tools cover almost everything. There are large metal tables and vials of CHEM everywhere. That side obviously belonged to Casteri. On the other side was a large computer made up of many small computers, all connected with CHEM. Crumpled up pieces of paper littered the floor like the remains of some great paper ball battle between the two of them, and strange electronic music that I didn't recognize poured from the speakers. That side had to have belonged to Marcus.

We all stood by the car that Casteri apprehended. It was completely revamped, I hardly recognized it.

Marcus and Lanker seemed to be going through and pulling a few more files before coming over.

"Is everyone ready?" I questioned, voice cracking slightly. I desperately tried to hide the fact I was a bit nervous about going to such a place. After realizing what it was, it was embarrassing to admit I was clueless about most of this.

From what I read, it was something like a rite of passage; most people have their first "experience" when they hit their teenage years.

"All ready Captain little man." Marcus gave me thumbs up before hopping in the driver seat. "I'm driving."

"Okay everyone, file in." I hopped in, while everyone else filled in the back. Thankfully, Casteri did a bit of expanding, and the back seats wrapped around the entire length of the car. I claimed the front seat while everyone else slid and adjusted themselves in the back.

"Drop the hatch for me, will ya?" Marcus called out to Casteri over the roar of the engine. The far metal wall was then dropped, giving us ample room to spread out and head to our destination.

"So, Captain, did you finally find out what a brothel was?" Tyrinie asked, with the same grin from earlier.

Not this again.

"Tyrinie, do you need to ride the rest of the way on *top* of the car?" I asked, the reddening of my face making my glare a lot less intimidating.

Tyrinie held up his hands in fake surrender. "Okay, I got it, no more talking. I mean, I know you're a little younger than me, but since you're from the West, I would've assumed you would have at least lost it by now. I feel like I should be calling you Captain *V*." I held my tongue as laughter erupted from the back seat, mostly between Tyrinie and Lanker.

I'm the captain; I have to be the mature one here. So, I was more than grateful when my favorite humanoid came to my rescue.

"Do not tease the captain, Tyrinie. I am sure you do not know as much about this as you think you do. You are still but a child yourself." Faylin responded, still nose deep in his book.

That definitely shut Tyrinie up as a chorus of "Oooo" and more chuckling flowed through the car.

Tyrinie's ears flaring and face red, yelled back. "What the fuck do you even know; I'm a lot more mature than you think. Plus, you're not even human; you don't know anything about this."

Faylin, calmly placing his book on his lap, gave Tyrinie what could only be described as a taunting smile. "You are correct, I am not human. However, I have been on this planet nearly 400 years longer than you have. There is plenty that I know, that you, as a child, have yet to learn."

Silence.

"Oh-oh! Taken down by the F-man!" Marcus cheered loudly, reaching back his hand to bump fists with Faylin. Even I couldn't keep my laughter down.

"Okay, quiet both of you." I called out before things got ugly in the backseat. "Let's focus on the task at hand."

"Actually, we don't have much time to figure out a plan, we're already here." Marcus pointed forward at the large and gaudy building that seemed to light up the night sky. The palace was huge, rivaling many of the buildings in the Southern region; a pale white with pink, blue floral decorations and gold trimmings. Large holograms surrounded the building and showed off pictures of beautiful humanoids, with the caption "Tonight's featured Teas" below. Men and women of all ages poured in the front doors by the dozen.

The car stopped and landed with a small thud as we began to climb out and adjust our clothes.

I took a deep breath and straightened myself up. "Let's go, team."

The doors swung open when we neared them, and I was immediately hit with the smell of perfume and…something sweet that I couldn't put my finger on. Many people milled around what I assumed was the lobby area. Some spoke to one another, while others sat silently, looking agitated or nervous.

A woman with impossibly long straw-colored hair stood at a host stand near the entrance.

I paused.

To my complete shock, she was clothed in nothing but a dusky gold and pink corset that left her entire chest exposed except for two heart-shaped stickers, silk underwear, stockings, and gloves. In fact, it looks like all of the workers wore similar uniforms, all in varying colors.

Already, I could feel my entire face heat up as I tried desperately to keep my eyes above her collarbone.

She gave a sweet smile, acknowledging our group. "Good evening gentlemen, I am called Chamomile. Please allow me to explain the levels of our facility." She pointed to a hologram next to her. "Level 1 has games and other forms of entertainment. Level 2 holds our many fine dining establishments. Level 3 is our entryway and lobby. Levels 4 through 8 hold our many collections of exotic teas, showrooms, as well as private rooms. Lastly, level 9 is the Throne Room for Madam Ginseng and her guests." She paused for a moment, giving us time to think. "Where may I send you today?"

I cleared my throat, but before I could respond, Tyrinie jumped in.

"We need to be placed on the list to speak with Madam Ginseng. It is an urgent matter, and I think she will find our information equally intriguing."

The woman seemed to pause at this, before nodding and pulling up a list. "As you wish, your number is 3,405, and your wait time in approximately 5 months. The fee comes to the total of 140,000 silvers.

I don't know what made me gag first; the number, wait time, or the cost. But to my surprise, Tyrinie didn't seem fazed. In fact, he seemed happily surprised.

He laughed. "Is that it?"

The woman nodded. "Yes, we are honoring the Dukas family discount."

Family discount?

Tyrinie clapped his hands together and smiled. "Beautiful, go ahead and place it on the Dukas tab."

"Of course, young Master. I will alert the Madam of your arrival."

Tyrinie nodded before grabbing my sleeve and pulling me away to the chairs in the lobby. "See, I told you I would take care of everything."

I admit, I was impressed, but that still didn't help the issue at hand. "That's great, but we don't have 5 months to waste."

Tyrinie laughed again as we all took seats, ignoring the stares around us. "Trust me, give it a few minutes."

Right as the words left his fangs, the elevator dinged, and two humanoids, male and female, walked out. The male was of average height and slender, with dark emerald hair that fell mostly in his face. The female was taller and heavily curved, with wild pale pink curls. Chamomile, looking directly at us, called out. "Master Tyrinie and company."

"And, that's our call." Tyrinie said with a smug smile. "Now that didn't take too long, did it?"

The one with the pink curls began speaking again. "I am called Jasmine, and this is Eucalyptus. We are the personal hands of Madam Ginseng and have been sent to bring you to her."

Angry shouts erupted from behind us, surely from patrons who have been waiting for far longer. But the two humanoids paid them no mind. "However, the Madam has given us strict instructions that she only wishes to speak with Captain Scarlet."

I froze. She only wants to speak with me? Alone? How did she even know that I was here? I never gave them my name.

Tyrinie seemed just as upset. "What! why just him?"

Eucalyptus nodded, speaking up. "Our Madam has given us orders to escort the Captain to her chambers. Meanwhile, she has instructed Jasmine and myself to lay out an assortment of our finest teas to entertain the Captain's crew."

Finest...teas?

I heard Lanker chuckle from the back. "You know, I don't really mind letting the Captain go by himself then." I shook my head, trying not to laugh myself.

Eucalyptus extended his hand towards the elevator, "This way please, Captain."

I walked forward slowly, my feet feeling heavier with each step. Before the door closed, I turned back to my crew. "Everyone, be on your best behavior."

"No promises!" Marcus replied, waving gleefully.

When the elevator doors reopened, I was staring down a dim hallway. The marble floors reflected the colors around them and seemed to glow with blue CHEM, making the walkway look ethereal.

The walls were made out of mirrors that were lined with gold trimmings and flowers. Chandeliers with pounds of crystal-like features decorated the ceiling.

It was completely silent, except for the soft music coming from inside of the walls.

"This way, Captain Scarlet." Eucalyptus held out his arm and guided me down the lit path and towards a pair of large deep blue doors. It looked almost as if I was walking directly into the ocean.

The doors swung open and revealed a large bedroom, with a sitting area towards the front. The bed was covered in shades of blue and a large sheer canopy top, with blue petals scattered on the floor.

There was a woman sitting on one of the larger chairs. She was calmly sipping from a large wine glass, watching me out of the corner of her slanted eyes. Her inky black hair was pinned up in an elaborate way, framing her thin, jewel-decorated face. She wore a simple golden dress that was covered by a long, silk, silvery robe that had roses staining the bottom like blood splatters. She was beautiful, that was for certain.

I tensed as the doors slammed behind me. She chuckled lightly, red lips still on the glass.

She stood and slowly waltzed over to me, hands in front of her as she gave a slight smile and bow. She looked a good few inches taller than me, with long legs that accentuated her even larger hips.

"My, oh my, you certainly have grown. Look at you; you look just as beautiful as your mother." She spoke in a breathy and melodic voice.

I shuddered at the thought, even though she was right. I, unfortunately, looked nothing like my father, but was a spitting image of my mother.

"Have we met before?" I questioned, still standing awkwardly in the doorway.

"Not officially." She chuckled again, before taking my hand and leading me to a chair. "But I do know of you, and I have *seen* you before, though I doubt that you remember."

"How do you know my mother then?"

She smiled, waving her finger back and forth. "Tsk, now that's not how this works. You are only allowed to ask me one question, my darling. That first question you asked was a gift, now you must play by my rules."

I sat back, fingers tightening against my legs as the room grew cold. "Rules?"

"Yes, here are the rules: You come in and ask me one question that you would like me to answer. In exchange, you will answer one question for me. When you ask me a question, I will answer it fully, and to the extent of my knowledge. However, no follow-up questions may be asked. Do you understand?"

"…yes."

There were so many things I could ask. I could ask her where father was. Or what was the secret to defeating Salem? But, right now, only one question needed to be answered, and that was the answer we came in here seeking.

"Where can we find Lelani Waves?"

She smiled, head tilting as if she was thinking. "Ah, I had a feeling you were going to ask that question. Unfortunately, I will not answer that question for you, not now at least."

"What? Why won't you answer it? That's all I need to know."

"Yes, I am aware you are looking for Lelani, but that is not where you need to be. In all honesty, Lelani…" She paused for a moment, staring directly at me with coldness behind her eyes "…would kill you and your team with no struggle."

I froze.

How was the daughter of an aristocrat such a danger? How did Madam Ginseng even know this? "You're lying."

"What would I gain from lying to you? I am telling you this for your benefit. You are going after Lelani to kill her, but you aren't strong enough to handle her, Scarlet. However, I will not leave you completely lost; I will tell you how to find Myrah Flynn in the North. She is the one you need to find first in order to start you on this journey. There is still a lot to this puzzle you are missing."

"What puzzle? What am I missing?"

She waved her fingers again, almost amused. "Remember rule number one, no follow up questions. I answered your question, now it is time for mine." She reached inside of her robe and pulled out an info chip, handing it to me. "This has the coordinates to Myrah's lair in the North. It is all you will need for now. Now, on to my question." She picked up her wine glass, taking a light sip as her hazel eyes bore into mine, almost as if she was trying to read me. "Why are you on this mission, Scarlet? What drives you to kill Lord Salem?"

I froze again. There was *no* way she could know about my mission. Only a handful of people knew about my creation, let alone my mission. But she...looked like she truly knew everything. Just by looking at her, I had the feeling I knew her, I could trust her, and I...wanted to tell her everything. She was a siren.

I blinked rapidly, trying to rid my brain of its fog.

"It's my mission; I was made to kill him. I can't...let my father down." Suddenly, I began to feel very sleepy.

"No no, that is not the reason. That is the reason Lyrik gave you. Tell me, Scarlet, what is your reason."

My reason? My reason was my father's reason. I was his weapon; I did whatever he needed me to do.

But...perhaps, there was something else. Something, in the corner of my mind.

"I...I don't know."

I wanted to please my father. I wanted him to be proud of me. Perhaps I also wanted to find someone who was like me. Maybe I wanted to kill Salem because I was afraid that...I could become like him one day. Salem and I are one and the same, both subjects of Project NaN.

But for some reason, one of us became the predator, and the other became the prey. We both believe that we are the predators.

"I need to know for myself." I responded without thinking.

"Hmm," She leaned forward, seemingly interested. "Need to know what for yourself, Scarlet? You must answer my question wholly."

"I need to know what I am, what makes Salem and I so different. And...what it is that Father isn't telling me." Father forbade me from ever reading him, or even touching his mind back when I had the ability to do so. But on some occasions, I slipped up, I found things that didn't match. I never wanted to question him, I figured he told me what I needed to know. But I always had this inkling I was missing something. "I want to know everything, and how I tie into this. I want to know about the nanoids."

After saying that, I felt a tugging on my mind, almost as if R was trying to tell me to stop. I tried, but it was no use. Thankfully, before I said anything else, she stood from her chair and began to walk over to mine. My head slowly bobbled downwards, partly from the sleepiness, and partly from the fear of staring directly at her again.

However, as she reached my chair, I felt her thin fingers slide along the side of my face before settling under my chin, lifting my face to look at hers. She said nothing as she slid her thumb across my bottom lip, opening my mouth slightly.

"You have been such a good boy, thank you for being honest with me." She whispered and gave me another soft smile, thumb pushing a bit farther and gliding along my bottom row of teeth. "In time, you will find exactly what you seek. But you must ask yourself, will you be ready for the answer when you receive it."

Get away from her, kid!

I heard R shout from the confines of my mind. I almost didn't recognize his voice.

She's no normal human. Get up!

An icy chill ran through my body as her thumb went deeper, running up and down my tongue. I couldn't get up, my entire body felt numb like I was in a dream.

"You must be very sleepy, come to my bed, I will allow you to rest for the night." Her hand slowed to a halt and she slowly removed her thumb from my mouth, a trail of saliva still connecting us. I shook my head, trying to regain some of my consciousness.

"I... can't, my team is waiting for me." There was no way I would spend the night here. Faylin was wrong on this one, this woman wasn't just a simple information broker, she was something else entirely.

"I will give your team rooms for the night, I'm sure they will not mind." She reached down and grabbed both of my hands, gently tugging me to my feet and leading me over to her bed. As we walked, I felt her unbuttoning my coat, sliding it off. When my knees hit the bedside, I stopped and turned around, coming face to face with the Madam.

Her eyes alone made my fingers go numb.

"I can't-" She cut off my words by lifting a finger to my lips.

"Sleep, my darling. Don't resist." She gave me a light shove onto the bed. As soon as my body hit the covers, I went completely slack. My body was...paralyzed.

I couldn't move. What's going on?

The red haze from my hands began to fizzle in and out as my eyes grew heavier and heavier. I barely felt her taking off my boots, and sliding me under the covers, caring for me as a mother would care for her child. Despite every reason I had to be afraid, I couldn't bring myself to be afraid of her. I felt calm.

I wanted to stay.

My eyes shut, and I drifted off into a light sleep.

I quickly came to consciousness as I heard the bedroom door open. The telltale sound of heels against the marble floor told me who came in.

The Madam.

She must have left after I fell asleep. I kept my eyes shut as she approached the bedside, feigning sleep.

I felt the bed dip as she crawled on my right side. She rolled me over to my back as I felt an even heavier pressure.

Was she was sitting on me?

My legs were trapped between hers, and her hands were flat against my chest. For a few moments, she didn't move, she just watched my face thoroughly.

After what seemed like an eternity, her hands began to slide upwards before finally coming to rest around my neck.

My neck? My breath hitched. Was she trying to kill me? Does she work for Salem? Do I jump up now, or wait to see what she's going to do?

I paused, holding back my urge to shove her away when she began to speak.

"I know you can hear me, R."

A cold chill ran down my spine. She was talking to R? How?

I felt her body shift as she leaned down close to my face, the smell of wine lingered heavy on her lips.

She planted a light kiss against my ear before whispering.

"Everything goes back to Xenon Tech."

For a moment, she just stayed there, face pressed into my neck almost as if she had fallen asleep. But soon after, she slid up into her previous position. I heard a slight chuckle come from her again.

"This is for you, Lady Xenon."

She slid off my body quickly, leaving me feeling cold, and exited the room.

I didn't see her for the rest of the night.

END OF CHAPTER 7

THE NURSE SHAKEDOWN PT. 2

I jumped up, looking all around me. What the hell happened last night?

I was still neatly tucked into the ocean blue bed, but all haziness and fatigue from the last night was gone. I felt like my normal self again, which made me question everything.

What was with that woman? I felt like I wasn't even myself, like I couldn't control my own body. If I didn't know any better, it was almost as if last night didn't even happen. But I know that it must have.

Bright sun rays entered in through the large arched windows, prompting me to get up. I needed to find my team; hopefully, they weren't too worried about me. I never planned on us spending the night. My coat was draped over the chair I sat in a few hours ago, and my boots were right below them.

I hopped up and stretched my arms, oddly feeling rather refreshed and relaxed.

I was about to leave the room when I realized what I forgot. "The info-chip!" It was sitting on the nightstand, right next to a note with a lipstick kiss mark on it.

Curious, I grabbed the note, picking up on the sweet yet earthy scent that came from it.

"I hope you enjoyed our night. Come back anytime."
Enjoyed last night?

Last night was confusing, to say the least. This woman was an entirely different kind of mystery. So many questions were left to ponder, so many possibilities.

I began thinking as I left the room, heading towards the elevator. How did she know who and what I was? How did she know my mother? What's the deal with Xenon Tech and who is Lady Xenon?

So many questions and no answers in sight.

The elevator ride was short, and I ended up back at the lobby, greeting the same flaxen-haired humanoid.

She greeted me with a nod. "Hello Captain Scarlet, I do hope you enjoyed your night. How may I assist you this morning?"

"I need to find the rest of my crew, do you know where I can find them." I asked, eyes following a few other workers.

"Yes, they can be found on Level 2, in our Tea Lounge. The Madam sent them down there to meet you."

"Thank you." I nodded politely as I ran back to the elevator, eager to see my group.

The Tea Lounge was a beauty. The entire room was bathed in hues of white and pink, gold trimming lining the areas between huge arch windows, and paintings of various angels on the ceilings.

The room was fairly quiet, save for the group of couches towards the back. Of course, the loudest people in the room were the ones I was looking for.

I surveyed my team as I sped towards them. They all seemed fine; they were all laughing and talking with one another. Even Faylin, the quietest in the bunch, was involved in the conversations.

"I assume everyone was okay last night." I popped up behind Faylin and Marcus, startling the latter, as choruses of "hellos" was said. "Well, well, well, look who finally decided to wake up.

Did the Madam make you pass out?" Tyrinie laughed, egging Lanker on.

"Welcome to the non-V club, Cap. You're a bit overdue, but hey, better late than never." Lanker jumped up, putting his arm around me. "Tonight, we have drinks, and you'll tell us the whole story. No skipping over dirty details, okay."

I gave an awkward chuckle, scratching the back of my head as Marcus and Casteri clapped for me.

"I hate to ruin the fun, but nothing like that even happened. We just talked." I had a lot of my own deciphering to take care of, but it was nothing that the entire team needed to know about right away. All that mattered was finding Myrah. "But we did get the information that we needed."

I held up the info-chip, handing it to Casteri. "The minute we get back to the ship, I need you to check out these coordinates."

"You got it, Captain." Casteri nodded, placing the chip in his wrist cuff.

"You are truly one of a kind." Tyrinie shook his head with an equally disappointed Lanker. "Who spends the night with a famous, beautiful Madam…and doesn't-"

"Okay, okay all other business aside. It's time to get back to work." I cut Tyrinie off. "We've had a rest, now it's time to go."

"Yes, Captain." They responded, sounding far from pleased.

"So Senna, is this where we say goodbye?" We just docked in the Seven Seas' hangar, when everyone began running back to their rooms. I told them they had thirty minutes to rest and get into uniform for a meeting in the War room for a debriefing.

"Yes, of course, I will be prepared to leave momentarily. What kind of responsible adult would I be to let you and your group trek back to your ship alone? I had to make sure you made it back alive." Senna responded, stifling a yawn.

"Whatever you say, because only crew members will be able to attend the debriefing."

"Trust me; I'm not losing any sleep. Let me just pack my things."
Senna left without another word, probably heading towards the
Med Bay.

I, myself, heading towards the War room, preparing what I was
going to say to the crew. Do we listen to Ginseng and go after
Myrah in the North, or do we stay in search of Lelani in the
South? Not only that, but what was the deal with Xenon Tech.
I've heard their name more than a few times before. But now,
there was no way it could've just been a coincidence.

How it ties in is the real question. Perhaps I would have to spare
another visit to Madam Ginseng.

I was nearly there when I heard voices flooding from the Med
Bay. Two voices, specifically. Curiosity led me to the edge of the
doorway, where I saw Marcus and a flustered looking Senna.

I leaned in, keeping myself hidden as Senna began to speak.

"Am I crazy, Marc? I must be for even considering this." Senna
ran one hand through his curls.

Marcus shook his head. "Nah, you're not crazy Senna, you're just
a very…caring person. Your reasoning is a bit crazy though."

What on Neutopia were they talking about?

"It's not crazy, Marcus. You didn't hear the way he spoke about
his family. It's no doubt his parents put this crazy notion in his
head. How else does a child get wrapped up in all of this?" Senna
leaned against the table behind him, crossing his arms. "He said
he wasn't close to his father or mother, he idolizes everything
about his father, and he's obsessed with killing our world's
leader. He thought I didn't notice, but he kept looking down and
fidgeting when he spoke about his parents, clear signs of lying.
Plus, his hands were covered in self-inflicted wounds. No doubt,
his parents must have abused him, neglected him at the least.
He's acting out because…he feels saving the world will give him
a sense of belonging, a sense of meaning. I can tell something
similar in Tyrinie, but he's a whole different story."

Marcus took a breath. "Listen, yea, the Captain is a bit 'different', but that doesn't mean he's crazy. He's driven, determined. Maybe, he just really wants to see some change in this hell-hole. It's not like our world is perfect."

"No, wanting to see change is…being involved in a few riots, or hell, joining the Rebel Guild and staying quiet. But this…this is a cry for help. And I…just can't leave him because of that. He needs someone who's going to keep him grounded, and hopefully talk him out of this craziness. Not to mention the fact he's very obviously ill, seriously ill. Between those blackouts and whatever is going on with his eye, he could be in more danger than he knows. "

Marcus shook his head again, taking a look at his watch. "So what, you're going to stay because you feel he needs you? That's unfair to both him and you. Sen, you do realize this will change your entire life, right? This isn't just something at a Rebel Medical Base."

"Don't you think I know that? I dedicated my life to helping those in need, and Scarlet falls in that category. What makes his life any less important than those I treat in the bases? Plus, it isn't like I can just go back to my normal life. I'm technically a fugitive. More or less, Scarlet is a special case. He's different, there is something he's hiding, and I won't rest until I find out all there is to know about him." Senna sat up, looking deep in thought. "Or, maybe it's just because he reminds me so much of Chastity, that I just can't stay away."

Marcus gave a sad smile, walking over and patting Senna on the back. "You're a good guy Senna, and your heart is in the right place. Just, think it over, will ya?"

Senna nodded before he and Marcus began heading towards the door. I jumped, and without thinking, sent myself teleporting into my room. I landed on the floor with a thud. Speechless.

"So…that's what he thinks, huh?" Senna thinks I'm crazy, and he wants to stay with me out of pity.

I raised my fist and slammed it into the floor, sending streaks of red through it. Damn him! I am not some child that needs protecting. I am more than capable of handling this on my own. Why did I even think bringing him would be a good idea? I stood to my feet, eyes leaking red haze as I stormed to the door.

"I'll show him, I'll let him know I don't need him." I grasped that doorknob.

"You might want to rethink that, kid."

I paused, mid-turn, as a familiar voice came through. I grimaced. "Long time no see, R. What brings you here?"

"Spare the sass, kid." R floated over, leaning against the wall right next to me.

"Can we not do this today; I really am not in the mood." It was taking everything in my strength not to break my door down. The haze from my hands began flooding past my feet.

"You really need to calm yourself down. What has you so worked up anyway?"

"What has me so worked up?" I spun towards him, teeth bared. "He thinks I'm some child, in need of saving. He thinks he needs to fix me like there's something wrong with me." My hands clenched tighter. "You heard him."

"Yea, I heard him. So why is that pissing you off?"

"Are you serious?" I paused, trying to take a deep breath. "I am so sick of him thinking I need him. He's been a thorn in my side ever since I brought him onboard; meeting me around every corner, trying to run tests on me like I'm some sort of freak. Hiding my powers from him is exhausting. I am so beyond anything he thinks he can do. Does he think that he can just waltz into my world…and *fix* it?"

R chuckled, much to my disdain. "So, you're mad at him for caring about you?"

"What? Why are you defending him?" I asked. R looked at me and rolled his eyes. "You think Persephone is the only one who has the right to care about you? Isn't that what makes humans different from humanoids?"

"Don't bring Mrs. P into this. This isn't about her."

"I think it might just be. Yea, the nurse thinks you're crazy. But let's go over your life for a second." R lifted his right hand, holding it flat, palm up. "On one side, you have your façade; a sixteen-year-old rebel-obsessed child who, is clearly having parental issues and knowing nothing about the real world, is trying to assassinate an all-knowing tyrant." He dropped that hand, lifting his left hand. "On the other side, we have your truth: You're an unplanned participant of an underground project which included injecting an unknown sentient cyber virus into your brain, turning your body into a walking test tube. Working for a disbanded, black-listed rebel group, you are now planning on assassinating an all-knowing nanoid-jacked tyrant." He paused, allowing this to settle in. "No matter which way you look at it, you look pretty crazy, and you need to be okay with that because even though you and I know the truth, they don't know."

I stopped to think. Did…my life really sound like that? I guess when it's said out loud, I did sound pretty...crazy. "So, what is it then? Am I crazy?"

"No, you're not. But hell, I'm just the figment in your imagination telling you that you're not crazy."

I gave a deep sigh, turning my back against the door and sliding down until I was sitting, head cradled between my knees. "Shut up, R."

I chuckled bitterly. "Senna is such an idiot; he's trying to fix me when I don't even understand me. I thought I had all of the pieces, but the further I go, the more I can't shake this feeling that something is missing. Of all times, why did Father have to go missing now?" I paused and looked down at my palm, the red wisps started to slowly dissipate. I guess I understood why Father never wanted me to ask questions, there was just too much to understand. I feel like I opened up Pandora's Box.

"R, you wouldn't lie to me, right? Can you tell me what's going on?"

I turned, but when I did, I realized I was the only one in the room.

I opened up the door to the War room, surprised to see the entire crew was already settled. I now had a team of six. My newest member, Senna, was sitting between a happy looking Marcus and Lanker.

I put on my best smile. "Well, look who's still here. What could this possibly mean?"

"You'll never believe it, Cap! Senna's gonna stay!" Lanker jumped from his seat. "I knew he would give in eventually, he just can't stay away from me."

Senna grabbed Lanker by his shoulder, shoving him back down in his seat. "Shut it, twerp. I'm not staying because of you. I, as a responsible adult, can't leave you children to your own devices. Plus, my father would kill me if I let you die. He actually likes you for some reason."

"Oh wow, my life is complete now." Lanker rolled his eyes. "Papa Angevine approves of me."

I shook my head; if keeping Senna meant dealing with the bickering every day...I might just need to rethink my decision. "Well, welcome to the team, Senna. Good to have you onboard." I gave him a nod as I reached the head of the table "On to more pressing matters, we have a bit of a dilemma to settle."

I grabbed the info-chip from Casteri, inserting it in the panel, allowing multiple documents to pop up. "The information I have is for Myrah, the northern member of The Management. After talking with Madam Ginseng, she made it clear starting with Lelani would be the wrong choice, and we are better off starting with Myrah and working our way down. We'll take a vote on what we should do." I paused, looking around the room.

"Everyone in favor of moving on to Myrah, raise your hand."

Tyrinie, Faylin, Marcus, and Lanker raised their hands.

"If Madam Ginseng thinks it's best to go to the North, we should listen." Tyrinie stated, picking at his claws.

"Okay, all in favor of staying."

Casteri and Senna raised their hands.

"Seriously? It's stupid to just get up and fly across Neutopia because of one woman's opinion." Senna shot back.

Tyrinie sat up. "Madam Ginseng is not just some woman. And Casteri put your hand down, what are you doing agreeing with this ass?"

"Excuse you!" Senna nearly jumped out of his seat.

I shook my head. "Moving on, I agree with Faylin and the others. Something just...gave me the feeling I should listen to her."

There was a lot about Ginseng that puzzled me, and if I ever got the chance, I would want to see her again and ask her another question. "Lanker, set full sail for the North. Casteri, Faylin, and Marcus, I need you three to cross Ginseng's information with the information we already received from the Western powerhouse. We still need to be completely careful. And Senna..." I grinned, eyeing our new member. "Since you are a permanent member of the Seven Seas Faction, you need to remove that pesky collar of yours."

"Woo! Time for Senna's initiation!" Marcus cheered along with Lanker.

I laughed, pushing back the nagging feeling in the back of my head.

Just barely out of the corner of my eye, I saw R standing in the doorway.

He was staring at me with an unreadable expression on his face.

END OF CHAPTER 8

Xenon Tech Massacre - Case goes cold

Xenon Technologies Lab: the leading pioneers in AI studies, CHEM development, and humanoid research. Established in 2465 by the esteemed Dr. Gene Xenon, Xenon Technologies took the world by storm by introducing the radical idea of creating vastly intelligent humanoids. After interviewing Dr. Xenon about his beliefs, this is what he had to say:

"Humanoids are perfect beings that we managed to create in an imperfect world. They have the potential to be far more than simple servants to the human race. Have you ever entertained the idea of what our world would be like if humanoids ran the banks, health care, even the government? I can tell you this...the human race would be in a much better place."

Ignoring the backlash that he received for his extreme beliefs, Dr. Gene Xenon continued to make great strides in Xenon Technologies Lab. One of his greatest accomplishments was developing the first batch of CHEM in 2467, which acted as a new and more powerful energy source for humanoids and humans alike. However, Dr. Xenon did not go public with his discovery until after the horrors of WWXII. The war ended in the year 2510.

Radiation poisoning was widespread, electricity was no longer a viable energy source, and the population dropped nearly 50%. After seeing that humanity was on the brink of extinction, Dr. Xenon introduced CHEM to the world; using it to reactivate all of the previously unresponsive humanoids. One by one, the humanoids began powering up and rebuilding society, dubbing the next hundred years the Golden Humanoid Era.

Much to the shock of the scientific community, in the year 2535, at the ripe age of 90, Dr. Gene Xenon went missing. No note or body was found, but after a year had passed, Dr. Gene Xenon was pronounced dead. His life's work along with the entire lab was left to his teenage prodigy son, Dr. Elias S. Xenon.—

The news article was damaged for the next few pages. I skipped through and jumped to the back, where the words became readable again.

--Dr. Elias Xenon, along with his colleagues worked on many projects within the walls of Xenon Technologies. Many of these projects had the goal of creating self-thinking and self-sustaining humanoids. One of these being, the companion humanoid.

Unfortunately, many of the secrets of Xenon Technologies will remain hidden. During the fall of 2600, the Xenon Technologies Lab was set aflame, consuming all of those who were inside. After believing that this was an unfortunate accident due to the nature of Dr. Xenon's work, an anonymous tip sent officers to the site of the fire. It was discovered that the scientists inside had been slaughtered before the fire was set. The incident was then dubbed, The Xenon Tech Massacre, and was investigated for months afterwards.

Out of the supposed 178 employees in the facility, only 174 bodies were recovered. Unfortunately, due to the fire damage to each of the bodies, none of them could be identified. The majority of the remains were found in the scientists' bunking area, few were in the lab itself, and one body was found in the main bedroom—

The rest of the article couldn't be read.

I placed the article on my nightstand and dimmed the CHEM lantern next to it, trying to get myself to fall asleep.

But...something seemed wrong.

"An AI lab...humanoid research...then a massacre followed by a fire to cover everything up?" Then, of course, there were the four unaccountable bodies.

Who were the people who made it out of the lab? And why? What did they see that night?

However, the question that kept popping in my head was the fact that Ginseng mentioned this place to me. Saying that, 'everything goes back to Xenon Tech'. What did that even mean...?

I sat up; obviously, sleep wasn't going to come tonight.

Tossing on my shorts and top, I made my way down to the hangar in the bottom of the ship. I needed to get some more information, and there was one place that I knew I could get it from. Hopefully, Marcus wouldn't mind if I used his computer for a little bit.

The crew was sound asleep from the snores I heard. "Perfect."

I crept down inside the hangar before slowly closing the creaking door and flipping on the lights. CHEM began to flow through the pipes, accompanying a light hum.

I headed over to Marcus' computer, taking a seat in the large padded chair before turning it on.

A simple smiling face appeared on the computer screen. It winked, and typed out: "Welcome back Marcus." Cute! I cracked my knuckles as an authorization screen emerged.

I had no clue Marcus coded this thing, so, I just needed to figure this out myself.

I allowed my hands to begin to glow as I placed them on either side of the computer. The haze began to flood around the large monitor, making fizzles and cracks of lightning in certain areas.

"Come on, let me in you dumb computer."

Soon enough, the smiling face appeared again, typing out: "Authorization code – disabled. Welcome, Guest."

That'll work for now.

It spoke again: "How may I help you navigate the cyber-net today?"

I typed back: "Search – Xenon Tech Laboratories."

The face did a little back flip before responding: "Search complete – multiple results found – click me to see your results."

I reached up and tapped the jumping yellow face. An image search appeared on the screen. The first few images seemed to be before the massacre: The grand opening ceremony, groups of scientists working diligently in stark white coats, and pictures of articles with announcements of various accomplishments. I scrolled down further, seeing a few darker images. One was of the lab after the fire: while the building itself was still standing, all of the windows were blown out and the walls were completely charred.

Scrolling a bit further, some of the bodies popped up. They were nothing more than bone and pieces of charred flesh. No wonder the officers couldn't identify any of them.

It was disturbing to say the least.

I scrolled through a few more images before switching over to a web search.

The face appeared again, typing out: "Search has brought up multiple results – care to specify?"

I thought for a moment before responding. "Search – Xenon Tech Lab location" Perhaps the lab required a bit of searching through, I doubt if much could be found…or even if it is still standing. But this might be a good lead.

"Search code – denied."

The words displayed in red across the screen. Denied? I changed my phrasing.

"Search – Xenon Tech Coordinates"

Again, the words "Denied" showed across the screen.

Why was the location to Xenon Tech a secret? The lab was destroyed centuries ago, nothing in there can be of any value? I went back to the image search, looking in the background of some of the images. Nothing looked familiar.

Of course, I wouldn't have expected it to. These images were taken before the Century War; this was still the old world. After the war, and the destruction and shifting of multiple landmasses, the lab could virtually be anywhere, if it was even still standing.

Who would know where it would be?

There was always Ginseng, but the more I thought about it, the warier I was about using her services again so soon.

I began typing again: "Search – database of pre-war artifacts." Surely, there had to be some sort of record kept for buildings that remained from the old world. Archeologists would have been more than adamant about making sure they stayed safe. Would they know?

Lady luck must have been on my side because one result popped up from my search.

"Results found – Children of Galaia."

The results popped up and images of people, young and old, donning white robes and strange markings filled the page.

Children of Galaia! I had never heard of such a thing. And what do they have to do with ancient artifacts? There was no additional information about the group, oddly enough. After scrolling further down the page, a certain picture caught my eye. I made the image larger, and tried to make out some of the words:

Further down, there was a picture of a large temple, with more writing beside it.

Sector 1.

Sector 1? If memory recalls, Sector 1 is in the Northern Region. This group sounded ominous. But if they were the only people who knew the location of the Xenon Tech building, then I would have to go and pay them a visit.

"The Children of Galaia!" Casteri sounded shocked as he popped his head up from his new invention. It looked a lot like a hover-cycle; sleek and silver, with glass veins of bright red CHEM running through like blood.

"Yea, have you heard of them. Their names popped up while I was doing some investigation." After jotting down notes and shutting down Marcus' computer, leaving it exactly how I found it, I went back to my office and did more research.

Apparently, they were a religious group that worshiped Salem, along with their 'deity' known as Galaia. Whatever structures and artifacts survived the Century War were deemed as sacred and documented in their temple. Of course, Salem seemed to be quite fond of the group.

"Most of those in the North knew about The Children of Galaia, but to be honest, they were more like a cult."

Casteri's tinkering stopped as he stood to crack his arms. He draped a neon blue tarp over the project before heading over to Marcus, flagging me to follow.

"Marcus, have you heard of this group?"

Marcus seemed to be in his own world, bobbing his head to the beat of music that poured through his black and yellow tinted headphones. Casteri leaned over and plucked them off of Marcus' head.

"Dude" Marcus yelled with a grin.

Casteri shook his head, dangling them in front of him. "Children of Galaia, ever heard of them?"

Marcus' face faltered for a moment before he tapped his chin, pondering.

"Yea, but what do you wanna know about them? Doesn't your kind hate their kind?"

Casteri paused for a moment before shaking his head. "It's for the Captain, not for me. I hold no particular animosity towards religious groups; The Children of Galaia have always unnerved me."

Marcus nodded before swiping back his headphones and turning back to his computer. After going through a few searches, he came across a bright red link.

He clicked it.

An odd picture popped up; it seemed to be some sort of family portrait. There was a man and woman, and in front of them were three children. Each of the children, two boys and one girl, had light blonde hair that faded to white, and crystal blue eyes. The mother had brown eyes that seemed to have dulled with time, and dark curls that rivaled my mother's. The father, or at least the man I assumed was the father, was a tall, large man that wore a large stark white robe and a...disturbing mask.

The mask was all white and resembled something that an old-world plague doctor would wear.

"Meet the head family of The Children of Galaia." Marcus pointed to the man in the mask. "The religion originated from the Xetyx tribe. Not much was actually known about this group, except for the fact they were rather secretive about their practices. That's the Tribe Leader; that is how all of his followers saw him. Nobody had ever actually seen his face. Supposedly he had taken an oath to never show his face to anyone other than their "Holy Matriarch". The Tribe Mother was the one who did most of the teachings, especially for the children. She also led all of their rituals along with her husband."

Casteri looked shocked for a moment. "You certainly know a lot about them, Marcus."

Marcus nodded with a smile. "My grandmother was a firm believer in the teachings of Galaia she would take me to their temple sometimes. My parents never cared much for her "crazy talk" though. I wouldn't say that I really believed it myself, but I did retain all of the information."

"Do you know where they meet?" That name...Galaia. I feel like I must have known it, because whenever I heard it, a shiver ran up my spine.

"Sorry Captain, but unfortunately that would be impossible." Casteri pulled up another link, this one holding a gruesome picture; children hanging from nooses while their parents lay slain on the ground in puddles of blood. "The tribe was massacred. It was quite a tragedy. Supposedly, enemies of the tribe, non-believers, killed off the head family along with the entire tribe. Not a single person was spared. The temple itself was destroyed shortly afterward, set ablaze. However, surely you aren't interested in their *teachings*. Their beliefs were pretty ridiculous; alternate dimensions, all-knowing creatures, and a secret gateway to their deity's realm."

Another mysterious massacre. Another piece of Xenon Tech's secrets buried.

Before I could respond, another voice droned out through the intercom.

"Estimated time of arrival to Northern Region, T minus four minutes."

I nodded and flagged Marcus and Casteri to the staircase.

The genocide of the Children of Galaia would have to wait; there was a member of The Management to deal with first.

END OF CHAPTER 9

THE MILITARY BRAT

I stood, coat tightened and sword firmly on my hip as The Seven Seas glided through the darkening gray sky.

The Northern Region looked exactly how I always thought it would: tall slate gray buildings with holograms on all sides, neon blue railways and walkways that weaved in and out, and large dark buses moving people all around. All of the people wore one of about five different types of uniforms. They neither laughed nor even spoke to each other on the street. The only sound came from the gusting wind and the rush of CHEM passing through the tubes. It was unnerving, to say the least.

It was nothing like the West, let alone the South.

"Go ahead and drop us on the outskirts, Lanker."

He nodded and the ship began to descend. We were nearly a mile out from the bridge that led to the gated region, and by the looks of it, a toll guard car was already on its way to our landing site. Perfect.

"Lanker, lower the ladder." I walked over to the edge of the ship as the rope ladder swung down, barely scraping the dirt below. Swinging my legs over the edge, I gripped on and fell at a breakneck speed, causing the guard's car to come to a screeching halt. I landed in a cloud of dust as the sound of a cocking gun filled the still air.

The others should have still been inside the ship, so I didn't have to hide this time

I cracked my arms, gathering red haze on my fingertips, as a burly looking man appeared behind the car door.

"State your name and purpose. You are flying an unregistered ship in unauthorized airspace."

I turned and began walking towards him as a red dot from his gun appeared on my chest. His finger methodically rubbed against the trigger.

I smirked and rushed forward, feet becoming nothing more than a blur of red. The man jumped, gun waving around as he looked for me.

"Down here." I waved, crouching down by his feet before I popped up and hit him square in the chest. Red streaks passed through him before he dropped motionlessly to the ground. I stood, dusting off my pants before dragging him off of the main road and into some nearby foliage.

I sat myself down in the passenger seat as the others made their way down the side of the ship. It felt nice to use my powers again, fighting with them felt so natural, like I was at home.

"How did you manage to obtain this vehicle, Mr. Scarlet?" Faylin asked as he sat behind the wheel. The others, donned in their uniforms, filled in the back.

"There was only one guard, and he was human, so I took care of things myself. It wasn't a problem." I replied, feeling quite proud.

"Well, I am glad that you were not harmed in the scuffle." Faylin slid on his seat belt and adjusted the mirror. "Do you know where it is we are heading?"

Before I could respond, Marcus rushed over and opened the driver's door.

"Sorry Fifi, not saying I don't trust your driving, but I think you better leave this to me. This is my home, and I do happen to know these streets better than anyone."

Faylin sighed before unbuckling himself. "As you wish, Marcus. You may drive." Faylin wedged himself in the back between Casteri and Lanker as Marcus took the front.

"Alright, is everyone buckled in tight?" Marcus yelled, popping on his yellow sunglasses that surged with the same CHEM power as his gloves. They all grumbled.

The engine veered to life as Marcus slammed on the gas, making all of our heads hit the back of the chair.

For a moment, as we cleared the forested area, most of the other squad cars didn't even notice us. There were about fifteen additional cars, four trucks, and numerous other soldiers standing by idly. The bridge was wide enough for us to fit, but only barely, and once we got inside, it looked like it was going to be an even tighter squeeze. The bridge would carry us from ground level to sky level within minutes. There were far too many twists and turns, and only a small railing keeping us on.

It looked dangerous, but taking the shuttle nearby would be even more deadly.

"Faylin," I called out as I turned uncomfortably in my seat. "I take it you have our coordinates already."

"Yes, Mr. Scarlet. After crossing the information given by Madam Ginseng, and the Western powerhouse, we have an exact location." Faylin reached up and handed me another info chip, this one slightly larger than the ones I had seen before. "There should be a slot near the steering wheel for you to input that."

I looked near the wheel, and sure enough, a slot was right next to a large blue light.

After plugging it in, a hologram of a map popped up on the windshield, nearly large enough to cover half of it entirely.

"Alright, looks like we're heading off to good ol' Sector 7. Shouldn't take too long now." Marcus said with a laugh as he shifted the car up another gear.

"I would recommend taking a deep breath before we get up too high. Most people have oxygen masks as they do this, but we will just have to work with what we have." Marcus yelled out as he rolled down his window, taking in a big gulp of air. We shook as the bridge passed beneath us, the chipped and dented metal in the road made us bounce uncomfortably. For a moment, the noise behind us became nothing more than a whisper.

I took a deep breath, keeping it steady as I rolled down the window and peeked my head out, causing my hair to whip around noisily. There was a thick layer of fog below us. It was so convincing...I felt like it would catch me if I jumped.

There were no birds here, nothing but fog, and the ominous drizzle from darkened clouds.

The closer the city came into our view, the further civilization seemed to get. With how densely packed the skyscrapers appeared, I doubted if anyone would've been able to follow us.

A sharp turn shifted us as we drove for a moment on only two wheels.

"Alright, and here we are!" Marcus shouted out as we leveled out back on even ground, now looking into the depths of the gray city.

The rain began to fall harder, showering everything with a deafening spray. It became harder to see, even with the speed of our wipers.

"Can you see where we are going, Marcus?" I rolled the window back up in a hurry.

"Barely, but I got it, no problem." He nodded, readjusting his sunglasses.

"Good, because I need you to get us as close as possible, and then into the nearest alleyway. We can regroup there."

"You got it, little man."

This powerhouse looked nothing like the one in the West, but more like one of the ornery displays in the Eastern Region shops. There were three large sectors: one on either side, connected to the largest sector in the center by bridges and wires.

Around the three sectors were numerous satellites and cameras. Each one was focused in a different direction and seemed to funnel in more information than I could fathom. We stopped in a dark alley, one that was hidden by the remains of a destroyed building, and further covered by the rain. Once the engine veered off, I began to hear everyone breathe.

"I never want to do that ever again." Senna whispered, looking greener than I remembered.

"Okay," I reached down and fiddled with the new wrist cuff that Casteri gave me. It came to life with a glow as a map of the area popped up. "This is our first true mission, is everyone ready?" The car was silent save for nods. I smiled.

"No need to worry, this will be a simple operation."

We had to split up; it would be our best chance. More importantly, finding a way to discretely use my powers when I found Myrah was a must. "Faylin and Marcus, you will both stay in the car and disable the CHEM control valves, cutting off power to the powerhouse. You will just need to join us after all of that is taken care of. Tyrinie and Casteri, you will both enter in from the west wing and make your way to the center. Lanker and Senna will be with me, we will start from the east wing and make our way to the center. Myrah is most likely in the center, so fighting our way there will not only weaken her forces, but it will make escaping that much easier. Understood?"

"Wait, shouldn't I stay in the car with Faylin and Marcus? I haven't had much time to practice with any kind of weapon." Senna questioned, sounding on edge.

"What's the matter, bro? Are you scared?" Lanker chucked whilst pulling his goggles tightly over his eyes. For once, those goggles would come in handy. The rain outside grew harder.

Senna rolled his eyes, but for once, didn't respond. Instead, he looked at me and awaited an answer.

If Senna was nervous, the chances of him getting hurt would just increase. Plus, if I only had Lanker, the chances of me being able to sneak and use my powers would greatly increase. Perhaps it was in my best interest to leave him here.

I sighed. "Sure, Senna will stay with Marcus and Faylin. After the power is cut, just stay in the car and wait for us to come back. You'll still need to keep a weapon with you, just in case this spot is discovered."

He nodded and fumbled with the pistol in his hand. "Got it."

I nodded. "Alright, if everyone is ready, let's get a move on!"

"Rah!"

The east wing of the powerhouse loomed above like a giant, it was absolutely breathtaking. My eyes narrowed through wet lashes as I called out behind me, breaking into a run. The gates were down, and from what I could see, the lights had been cut off, only emergency light filled the building.

Perfect.

"Are we ready Lanker?" I pulled out my sword in a whip of red, the engraved symbols beginning to glow.

"You got it! I'm pumped up." He was bouncing from foot to foot, grinning madly.

I nodded, the same excitement coursing through my veins.

In a mad dash, we stormed the doors.

Intruder alert: Door 4A – Eastern Wing. Repeat: Intruder alert.

Sirens blared as red lights began to grow, casting the hallway in a dim glow. We continued forward, keeping our eyes sharp for any guards. So far, none were spotted.

It wasn't more than five minutes when the intercom spoke again.

Intruder alert: Door 7B – Western Wing. Repeat: Intruder alert.

Tyrinie and Casteri were right on schedule.

"Heads up, Cap. I think we got company!" Lanker called out as we turned another corner. Behind us, down the next corridor, roughly six soldiers were on our tail.

This would be easier if I handled it on my own. "Lanker, continue ahead, I'll meet you around the next hallway."

"What, are you crazy, Cap?" Lanker shouted, grabbing onto my forearm before I turned around.

"That's an order, Lanker. Trust me." I tried to give him a reassuring smile as I tugged my arm out of his death grip. "Now go."

He nodded reluctantly and headed down the next hall.

I turned and headed back.

Listening closely, I heard six pairs of heavy boots making their way to my location. I smiled, reaching up and cracking my arms again.

"Alright R, let's show them what we can do." I attached my sword to my hip before closing my eyes and allowed my barriers to drop, feeling warmth spreading down my body like fire. Wisps of red came from my eyes and my fingertips as I bounced on my heels, waiting for them to appear around the corner.

Finally, they were before me, four men and two women. The man in front seemed startled, whispering to the soldier next to him for a moment.

"What the hell is that, Jenkins?" He spoke, eyes never leaving me.

Jenkins seemed just as confused.

I gave a quick smile before crouching down and zipping towards them as I did to the guard in the forest.

"Open fire!" I heard Jenkins yell.

Too late.

I grabbed the first person to my left, hooking my arm around his neck before slamming my palm into their gut, streaking their body in red before dropping them. I ran for the next one to my left, connecting my fist straight to their chest, before hopping to the next. And then the next. Until they were all on the ground, unmoving, and painted in streaks of red that were slowly fading. I gave a breathy laugh before calling R back. I didn't feel exhausted this time around. In fact, I felt even more energetic. I turned and rushed forward to find Lanker.

To my surprise, Lanker was only a few corridors pass where I left him. He seemed surprised to see me.
"Thank goodness!" He punched me in the shoulder. "You're a wild one, ya know that."
Thankfully, Lanker hadn't hit much trouble. I only spotted a few guards that were now littered with holes.
"Let's keep moving." We continued into our run as I called into my earpiece. "What is your status Casteri?"
There was crackling on the other line. "Guards - - position - - fire - - over."
"I couldn't hear that Casteri, repeat!"
The line was dead.
"Faylin, do you copy?"
"Yes, Captain." He responded, only a tad bit fuzzy.
"You and Marcus head over to Casteri and Tyrinie's position. Senna, continue keeping the power off, just like how Marcus was, Copy?"
"Copy" Faylin responded before the line went dead.
"Do you think they are alright?" Lanker asked with the slightest bit of panic in his voice.
"Trust me I don't think anyone could take Tyrinie out. They're fine." If there was anything that I trusted in Tyrinie, it was his tenacious attitude. "Let's continue."
I cut down the last guard that was standing in front of the entrance to the bridge that led to the main corridor. The bridge seemed to go upwards and head towards a staircase. The staircase itself seemed to lead right to the roof.
The roof, which must've been where she was.

The bridge itself was glass with a glass tube around it. Just walking through made me feel claustrophobic.

"Are you ready for this, Cap?" Lanker asked, his voice a bit horse from shouting.

"More than ready" I looked up, and to my surprise, R was standing at the end of the corridor, right near the base of the staircase.

I looked at him out of the corner of my eye, not saying anything. His face was weird. Unlike the times when I swore he didn't know when to shut up, this time, he didn't say a word. He just stared, unmoving.

Finally, as I was passing him, he spoke.

"Be careful, kid. This is when it all begins." Even the tone of his voice was unrecognizable.

I stopped and turned, but he was already gone.

"You alright" Lanker questioned, hand already on the doorknob.

"Yea I'm fine. Let's go."

After making our way up the dark staircase, we came face to face with an even darker sky. While the rain seemed to have slowed down, it still made quick work of plastering my hair to my face. I pushed it back to the best of my ability.

"Captain" Lanker stood by me, finger ready on the trigger of his gun. "I think that's her."

On the opposite end of the roof stood a woman. She was facing away from me, feet dangerously close to the edge.

I stepped closer, sword hand gripping tighter. "Are you Myrah Flynn, a member of Salem's Management?"

Even though I had to scream over the pounding rain, my voice barely sounded like a whisper.

She wore the uniform of a military official; dark green skirt, impossibly heavy looking boots, and a black jacket that now hung loosely from her frame. She turned and looked at me with cold, unmoving golden eyes. Her face was framed in blonde locks that barely dusted over her shoulders.

"And who might you be?"

Her voice made the roof tremble. It was soft, yet terrifying. She was nothing like the guards down below; she had the look of a true killer.

I squared my shoulders and walked closer, sword pointed directly at her. "I am Captain Scarlet of the Seven Seas, avenger of Discordia." I took a deep breath, parting my feet. "Because of your allegiance with Salem and your many crimes done under him, you will die today."

I watched closely as she studied my face. She eyed Lanker, who was standing close behind me, watching the door closely.

"You are the wanted child, yes? From the West" She spoke motionlessly, hand grazing along the wet, metal railing.

"Yes." I pulled my coat out of the way, showing her my red collar. She paused, looking surprised for a moment. "I do not, and will never follow Salem. All who follow him, and all who stand in my way of destroying him, will die as well." I couldn't stop the smirk from covering my face, this felt all too right. I continued. "Do you have any last words?"

She smiled, "Such big words from such a small boy." Her hand clenched the railing. "I must say, you are remarkably brave. Discordia should feel lucky having you fight for them." Her eyes narrowed as they became a tad lighter. "But you are also a fool. And I will not have a rebel in my presence threaten the name of our great Lord Salem."

Within a moment, her hand twitched and a long metal rod was ripped from the railing. She pointed it at me, copying my stance. "Today, Captain Scarlet is the day *you* will die." She opened her eyes again and streams of golden haze began leaking from her eyes and her palms. There was a flash of white as the haze from her hand made contact with the metal, and a horrid twisting noise resounded.

I covered my ear with my free hand as I stared forward. The rod that was in her hand had twisted and became a large and impressive sword, bathed in a golden glow.

I froze, lips becoming cold.

What the hell?

Was this woman...like me?

"What the hell was that, Cap?" Lanker seemed just as startled as the door behind him busted open, more guards coming up.

"Focus, Lanker! You take the guards, I'll take Myrah." I nodded at him, before charging off towards Myrah.

I flexed my fingers. "Let's go, R."

END OF CHAPTER 10

11

THE GOLD SOLDIER

T hunder clapped as our swords collided. Streaks of crimson and gold filled the sky like synchronized fireworks. Myrah was quick on her feet, barely staying in one spot for more than a moment. I could barely land a hit with my hand, let alone my sword.

I jumped back, swearing as her sword nearly missed me again. It was practically the size of her entire body, and yet she manipulated it as though it weighed nothing. I pushed the hair out of my eyes again, charging forward, sword at the ready. The marks began to glow as the haze filled my eyes.

Clash!

We met in the middle; our swords flush against one another, breath heavy with mist and sweat. I spun under her in a flash, aiming a kick at her stomach. I barely made contact before she jumped back. Red streaks fizzled through her skin for a moment before fading out.

"It didn't work." I murmured in disbelief. When my barriers are down, a solid hit from me would paralyze and often shut down the nervous system of my opponent. But she brushed it off as if it was nothing.

She cracked her neck before looking back at me. "That hurt a bit." A grin cracked across her face as she charged towards me again. "Let's see if you have the guts to do that again, little boy!"

I jumped back as she advanced dangerously close, nearly losing control of my sword as her attack sliced across my bicep.

"Ack!" I froze as my arm went completely numb. The wound had gold wisps coming from it like flames and traveled down my veins in lightning bolts.

"Damn it." I tossed my sword into my left hand, the feeling just barely coming back into my right.

I met her again as we clashed. I risked looking back for a moment at Lanker, and thankfully, he wasn't alone. Marcus, Casteri, and Lanker stood in a triangle formation, taking out an onslaught on guards.

Faylin and Tyrinie must have been below. My whole team was set and accounted for. The thought gave me peace of mind.

I whipped my head back, only to find that Myrah was gone.

"What the-" I looked to my left and right, but she had completely vanished.

I paused, feeling the wind shift just a tad, before jumping and tumbling to my right. She had come from behind, and I nearly missed a sword in the back. I mentally berated myself for my carelessness before standing back to my feet.

It was about time to end this.

I charged forward, feet becoming a blur as I slammed full speed into her, knocking her back. Time seemed to slow down as I whipped behind and charged again, this time sword at the ready. She turned, barely having time to raise her sword before mine connected with her neck, and sliced through completely.

There was a sickeningly wet thud as her body collapsed in a pool of blood, her head just a few feet away.

For a moment, she stared at me, mouthing something through bloody lips before her eyes went blank. Her hand, still tightly gripped around her sword went slack, and her sword became a hunk of metal once again.

I dropped my sword and looked up at the sky before looking down at her again.

The rain was washing away the evidence, sending it flowing down off the roof and down the front of the building.

"It's over." I grabbed my sword, attaching it to my hip before reaching for her head, grabbing it by the hair.

The other guards stopped attacking when they saw me some began to back up in apparent fear.

"Your boss is dead, if you want to live, I would leave Now"

Their weapons dropped, and they hurried one after the other down the dark staircase, leaving only my team on the roof. I was far too tired to chase after them.

Everyone was silent except Marcus, oddly enough, who breathed a sigh of relief.

"Thank goodness that's over." He wiped his soppy wet locks out of his face and made his way over to me. "Looks like you're hurt again, little man."

The cut went right through my coat and tore through layers of flesh. It was painful, no doubt, but I could already feel my body working its magic.

"Yea, it's alright though. You okay?" I began heading towards the others. And for a split second, I swore I saw fear in their eyes.

"Yea I'm good, little man. Though I can't say the same for Myrah." Marcus looked at the decapitated head. "The crazy broad put up one hell of a fight."

"She did." Her powers rivaled my own. It was confusing...unnerving even. Salem and I were the only ones in existence who were supposed to have powers like that. Where did hers come from?

"Marcus, grab her body." I paused as we reached the others. "Head back to the car with it; we'll take it aboard and study it further."

"Uh...yea sure. You got it."

As Marcus headed off, I looked into the eyes of Lanker and Casteri with a smile. "We did it, guys."

Lanker dropped to the ground dramatically. "Thank the Maker! I thought I was seriously going to die for a second there."

Casteri shook his head and laughed lightly.

We really did it. The first member of the Management was dead. Now, I needed to make sure Salem knew it.

After exiting the roof, we followed the adjacent staircase which led deeper into the powerhouse's levels. From Ginseng's info-chip, this was Myrah's office. Apparently, all of the broadcasts for traitors and executions were sent out from this very office.

I smiled. We were about to send off a very different message.

Her head, still firmly in my grasp, knocked against my boot with every step I took, making a dull thud. The blood was staining my pants.

"Mr. Scarlet. Do you read me?"

The chipped noise fizzled through my earpiece. But I was more than happy to hear the sound.

"Hey, I hear you Faylin. Are you and Tyrinie okay?"

The line went dead for a moment before it fizzled back.

"Yes, we are okay. Would you like us to meet you in a certain location? Or should we regroup with Senna."

While I would have loved to have them here, leaving Senna alone for too long might not be the best idea. He might need some backup.

"Go ahead and head back to Senna. We will meet you there in no time."

"Copy that, Captain."

Senna would be more than safe with Faylin around, that's for sure.

The door before us was large and foreboding: a dark slate color equipped with a retinal scan.

Perfect. I held her head up to the pad, a neon blue light popped on and scanned through her dim eyes.

"Welcome back, General Flynn." A robotic voice droned out.

"Thank you." I muttered under my breath. The office was huge, exactly how I expected it to be. With pillars in all corners and a large rug with Salem's emblem engraved. In the corner stood a large metal platform that had blue particles flying upwards, almost like an invisible cylinder.

There was a camera floating in front of it, seemingly off for the time being.

"Let's go boys." I sped over to the platform and stepped inside cautiously. The air was warm, and a bit stuffy.

"Um, what are you doing, Cap?" Lanker asked, sitting on top of Myrah's desk.

"I'm just going to give society a bit of a message. Casteri, turn that camera on for me please." I brushed my coat down, attempting to wipe some of the blood off. No need to look like an absolute maniac.

Casteri clicked the button, and another automated voice came on. *Welcome, General Flynn. You will be live in 5, 4, 3, 2, and 1."*

There was a dinging noise, and I cleared my throat.

"Attention all of Neutopia, I am Captain Scarlet, leader of the Seven Seas faction. Today, I'm letting everybody know that the threat of executions is now gone." I held up Myrah's head, showing it to the camera, making sure they all got a good look. Lanker looked over at me in shock.

"General Myrah Flynn, servant to Salem, and head of all executions distributed by the North, has been killed." I lowered it back down. "Let this be a warning. All of those who work under Salem will die. And then, Salem himself will die. I am here to finish Discordia's work. I will kill Salem and bring freedom to Neutopia."

I nodded, and Casteri hurried and turned off the camera.

Lanker let out a breath. "Was that a good idea, Cap? That was pretty intense. We can be sure Salem will be on our tail now."

"Good." I slung Myrah's head over my shoulder. "I want him to know we're coming for him."

I flashed him a smile. "Alright, grab what you can, and let's head out of here.

"Are you out of your mind, Scarlet?" Senna cringed and slid to the other end of the car when Marcus entered with Myrah's body. "Why are we taking a dead body with us?"

"I told you already Sen, the girl was maxed out, so we gotta check out her body. Who knows what kind of drugs she was pumped with?" Marcus explained as he buckled her body up, wedging it between himself and Senna.

This was in no way the work of drugs. It was almost as if she was like me, like she had a nanoid like me. But that was impossible. From what father said, only two nanoids were pulled from cyberspace and experimented on; E and R. E was placed in Salem, and R was placed in me. So if it wasn't a nanoid, I had no idea who, or what, was inside of her.

I took a seat, slumping slightly due to the exhaustion and realization that was now settling in. Persephone saw that broadcast. Emme saw that broadcast. What do they think of me now? Is father proud right now? He should be, this is what he wanted me to do.

This was my job.

Marcus started up the car, and I could barely hear Lanker and his tales of grandeur, reciting every single thing that happened. Tyrinie was upset he missed everything, claiming Casteri got them lost. Faylin stayed silent, and Senna was still trying to get as far away from the headless body next to him. I stared at the woman's head in my lap; her eyes were still more than halfway open. They were looking back at me. Her graying tongue was just barely poking out from her bloody lips.

I took my thumb and pushed it back in her mouth, feeling along her teeth, just like how Madam Ginseng had done to me.

Her head was making my lap cold.

The trip out of the city was smoother than the trip in. All of the guards had been re-stationed inside the city in order to look for the ones responsible for General Myrah's death. Slipping past was easy, especially since we were in one of their own cars.

The Seven Seas was still standing proudly in the forest, drenched from the now-passing storm. We filed out and, one by one, headed up the ladder and back on board.

Tyrinie yawned loudly, exclaiming he was too exhausted to do anything further and excused himself to his bunk rather quickly. Faylin, Casteri, and Marcus began moving Myrah's body down to the lab to do experiments before rigor mortis set in. Senna hurried off to his office, still traumatized by the car ride.

I grabbed my things, including the head that I had grown quite attached to, and went into my quarters.

It had been days since I last messaged Persephone. She must have been worried sick by now. I sat down at my desk, placing Myrah's head next to the lantern and grabbing the AT cypher. There were no new messages.

I began to type:

Mrs. P,

Sorry for the absence. I have been busy with the team. Everything is moving so fast, I can hardly keep up. Has father come back home yet? I wish that I could tell you what was going on, but I can't. I don't want to put you or Emme in any danger. Do me a favor...if anyone asks you if you know me, say "no". This will all be over soon. I promise.

Scarlet

I felt like there was so much more that needed to be said, but I just shook my head and sent it off before I changed my mind. It beeped.

I sighed. "Yes, R?"

I heard a breathy laugh coming from my bed. R had stretched himself out over my covers.

"Look at you, sittin' over there looking like a real rebel. Daddy would be proud." He crossed one leg over the other, kicking it back and forth. "And when are you going to get rid of that head, it's gross."

I looked over at Myrah's face.

"That doesn't matter." I reached over and smoothed down some of her hair, it felt strange between my fingers. "What was she? And don't say that you don't know, because I know there is so much you aren't telling me right now."

I glared at him, facing him completely. "What's really going on, R?"

He continued to stare at the ceiling. "I don't have to tell you anything. Your boys are going to figure it out in a few minutes."

"What?" I paused, looking towards the door as if someone was going to waltz in.

"They are testing Myrah's body right now, and they are going to find she wasn't entirely human. They are going to call you via intercom in about four minutes. Her insides are completely corrupted, destroyed."

"Corrupted...like a computer? What does that mean? Is she a humanoid?"

He shook his head. "No, she *was* human at one point in time. But, you'll see everything else very soon."

I got up and stormed over to the bed.

"No, tell me everything, R!" I grabbed him by the forearm. It was warm and so smooth I thought my grip would slip. Little bits of code flew off from where I grabbed him.

He looked at me, a calm and even expression on his face. "The Hybrid Theory."

My grip loosened. "The…Hybrid Theory? What's that?"

I remember that we grabbed some papers that mentioned something about a theory. It was from the Western powerhouse. Even something in Myrah's powerhouse mentioned a theory

"It's Salem's project. His key to immortality. You have the papers, why don't you read through it yourself instead of begging me for the answers."

My eyes narrowed. "I'm not begging you for answers. I'm just sick of you hiding shit from me. Why didn't you tell me Myrah wasn't human?"

"I think you're mad at daddy for not telling you that, not me."

I paused. "Well...why do you keep pulling me into that weird red world, cyberspace, or whatever the hell it is!"

Surprisingly, he froze at this. "What do you mean?"

"What? D-don't act like you don't know. I have those terrible pains, my eyes start bleeding, and then when I wake up, I'm in this weird red world. My clothes, the trees, the grass, everything is different there."

I barely finished my sentence before R jumped up, grabbed me by both biceps and held me still. My feet were inches off the ground.

"What are you talking about, who did you see? Tell me everything, Scarlet!"

My breathing got faster as I tried to wiggle out of his grip.

"I-I don't know, I thought that you were doing it to me."

"Me? Of course not" He yelled with a bitter laugh. "I would never take you there. I don't even have the power to do that. Who did you see?"

"No one. I'm always by myself. I-There is a voice I hear, but I never see him, he's always behind me."

R focused on my face, not even breathing. I was lowered down.

"Listen to me, Scarlet. If you ever go back to that world, you tell me right away." His eyes were blazing. I had never seen him like that before. "Understand?"

I nodded my head, backing away from him. "Gotcha."

He took a deep breath, gaze now looking back at Myrah's head. His lips were tight.

Within the next blink, he was gone.

Before I could even think about going to sleep, I heard the crackle of the intercom.

"Captain, you are needed in the Lab, Captain to the Lab. Thank you!

END OF CHAPTER 11

12

CORRUPTED BEAUTY

I rushed down to the lab as quickly as I could, nearly tripping in the process. The lab wasn't too far, it was right across from Casteri's workshop and Marcus's computer room. Apparently, Casteri and Marcus set the lab up for Faylin so that he could have his own little office. With those strange books with symbols and his apparent knowledge for CHEM tech, I couldn't think of a better idea.

The door zipped open as I walked closer, revealing my three crew members donning lab coats, goggles, and gloves. They were all standing a few feet away from the table that now held Myrah's exposed body. Her chest had been opened up, along with her stomach.

"I'm glad that you could join us, Captain." Casteri greeted me, eyes not leaving the body on the table.

"Sure, no problem. Is everything alright?" They all looked terrified. Even Faylin looked unnerved.

"Perhaps you should see for yourself." Faylin came forward and pulled me by the sleeve until I was right next to the table.

I felt bile rise in my throat and had to force myself not to vomit. I didn't know what was worse, the sight or the smell.

Her insides were worse than the picture R put in my head. It was horrendous. A terrible black ooze flowed through her body, covering all of her organs, making it look like a stew of black tar. But her organs were the strangest part; they were completely black with bluish vein-like marks. The blue marks were also on her ribs, and on the inside of her flesh. It looked as though something came into her body and...and

Corrupted her.

Was this what corruption looked like?

What could have done this to her?

I stepped back and looked at the others. Their faces mirrored mine. "What do you think this is?"

For once, Marcus didn't have a witty remark. He simply shook his head, mouth agape.

"I have no idea, little man. I...have never seen anything like this. I knew that Myrah was...strange. And yea, maybe I thought that she was a bit inhuman, but I never would have thought this."

I shook my head, gathering my thoughts. "Faylin, go to my office and grab all of the documents that we have on the Hybrid Theory. Marcus, go in your database and pull out everything you have stored about the Hybrid Theory. Meet Casteri and I in the War Room."

They all nodded as I exited. Even if it took all night, we would find out what Salem did to Myrah Flynn.

"None of these documents are making any sense. These scientific calculations are completely ludicrous." Casteri murmured, stifling a yawn as he looked through another page.

Hours passed, and the War Room table was filled to the brim with files and papers, holograms and emails. Faylin, Casteri, Marcus, and I each took a corner of the table, trying to decipher the mess.

"By the looks of it, someone was trying to create a human-humanoid hybrid creature. Fusing both kinds of DNA." Marcus looked through another file, handing it to Casteri. "This would never work, right?"

"Humanoid DNA and Human DNA aren't compatible. That's the main reason why a humanoid male cannot impregnate a human female. It's like mixing oil and water." Casteri answered.

"Not only that, but various strands of humanoid DNA are toxic to humans. Our bodies run solely on CHEM, a few grams of CHEM would be enough to kill a full grown adult." Faylin sat up and walked over to my side of the table. "Mr. Scarlet, look at this. Despite the obvious flaws in this plan, I think I know what the purpose of this endeavor might have been."

The paper held a diagram of a human body that had humanoid parts overlapping it. On the sides were scribbles of notes filled with possibilities if these two were to merge. Most of the notes were blurred due to age, but a few could be read.

Cell Regeneration

Enhanced Physical Abilities

Complete Self Preservation

Decreased need for substance

Immortality

My eyes focused on the last entry. Immortality. Is that what they were after? R's words came back to me.

Were they trying to build something...like me?

Faylin rubbed his chin, holding the paper high. "It looks like someone was trying to build their own super human."

I shook my head. "Not just that, they were trying to become immortal."

All other talk stopped. Casteri looked over at more of his pages. "Impossible. There's no way it would ever work."

"I know. But somehow, someone thought they had the right concoction with Myrah, and look what it did to her. And..." I paused for a minute, throat going dry. "You remember what Lanker said, about how her hands could manipulate metal, and how she looked stronger than any other human.

Perhaps science was wrong on this one. Even if she wasn't immortal, it sure did *something* to her."

Casteri ran his hands through his hair before diving back into the papers.

"Okay, let's think of this practically." Marcus tossed his stack of papers down before walking towards the center of the room. "I'm a human, and this theory is saying I can just inject some humanoid DNA into my veins and become a super human, right?"

Faylin sat on the edge of the table next to me, crossing his legs. "Correct, but we know it cannot be that simple. That would never work; it would kill the human host."

Marcus nodded. "Okay, good. So what would make that not happen with Myrah?"

I popped my head up. "Maybe someone found the right concoction? Maybe they were able to, I don't know, fuse the genes and balance it perfectly."

Faylin shook his head. "Still no. As Casteri said, humanoid DNA and human DNA cannot mix. It would not work. If that were so, there had to have been a third ingredient, something to bind the fusion."

"That's because they didn't just find the perfect mixture, they found the perfect host." Casteri looked pale as he bore his eyes into the screen before him. "The Hybrid mother"

The Hybrid Mother?

We all waited for Casteri to read the file.

He cleared his throat. "It's an email. I'm deciphering who sent it. This was sent directly to Salem. This is old though, this email was sent February of 2610."

"That's nearly 400 years ago." Disbelief was heavy in my voice.

"I know. This wasn't even pulled from any files we took from the powerhouses. Marcus pulled this folder a few nights ago using his own techniques, we hadn't opened it yet. Here, listen to this:

"I have done it. After many failed attempts and trials, I have created the serum. Of course, the idea of the host came straight from you, and it was a work of true genius. After nearly a week of trying to keep the host alive, I have stabilized them, and the hybrid serum is pumping through their veins as we speak. The perfect balance of H-DNA and DNA, along with the catalyst from you, my Lord. I have created the hybrid mother; the vessel will stay with me in the lab as I perform more tests. I will inject myself with the serum at once to test the effect. It should be everything that we expected and more. We are one step closer, my Lord."

Dr. Cyryl Plaski

The room grew still and cold.
The immortality that R said Salem was after...wasn't for himself. Father already told me that I would stop aging in a few years, once my body fully matured. Salem must be the same way given the fact that he has been alive for so long. He's already immortal. This serum - was for his followers. And this Doctor Cyryl seemed to have the key that Salem needed.
Myrah Flynn wasn't an experiment; she was a candidate.
Marcus was the first to speak. "He's building an army of...genetically enhanced humans?"
I nodded. "*Built*, is more like it. This email is centuries old, this production has been going on for longer than any of us could've known. Who knows how many more of these creations are walking around with this serum that turned them into monsters?"
What was the "catalyst" that was mentioned?
"Just how long have these people been trying to play God?" Marcus asked nobody in particular.
What has Salem created?

"New plan, team." I spoke as I stood to my feet. "Our first priority is finding this "Hybrid Mother" and destroying it. Salem cannot be left with such a dangerous serum."

"But what about the Management?" Casteri asked.

"What's the point of chasing them all down when Salem can create more like them with a simple injection? This production needs to stop now. As I said, we have no clue how many of these hybrids are running around."

Father, did you know about this as well?

"Right now, Salem has his own personal lab rat hidden with Dr. Cyryl. We will find it, and destroy it."

She fought just like me. She had powers just like me. Her attacks had the same effect on my body that my attacks had on her body. There is no doubt about it, humanoid and human DNA weren't the only things used in that experiment.

Nanoids were used as well.

How they were used, and who knew about them being used was still up in the air. But the nanoid threat was very real, and this situation was going from bad to worse. Nanoid DNA was being passed around in a syringe. Anyone who came in contact with it would become like Myrah.

They would become like me.

I couldn't tell the others about that. It would risk exposing the nanoid world and cyberspace. And that would only be one step from me being discovered.

The only option was to find this Dr. Cyryl, find the hybrid mother, find all others who came in contact with that serum, and destroy them all.

Bury everything.

Nanoids must never be discovered.

I looked over at the tightly sealed glass container that Myrah's head was now sitting in. Her face had begun looking more purple than before, and it started to smell.

Now, she was sealed and the container was filled to the brim with CHEM fluid. I flicked the container, making the head wobble a bit. What was she trying to tell me in her last few moments?
She mouthed something, but I couldn't figure it out.
Maybe she was cursing me.
Maybe she was warning me.
So much needed to be done, and my time was running shorter than I thought.
I stood and walked towards my bed as my head began to ache. It started off as a dull throb, but then made its way to becoming unbearable. I groaned and slid myself under the covers; face flush against the pillow as I began to tremble. Was it happening again? The room began to spin. I shut my eyes tightly as blood began to rise from my throat.
Just breathe; it'll be over with soon. I knew I had to keep myself calm.
I looked over to my side as my vision went black.
I saw Myrah looking at me.

I turned my head and felt grass against my face. My eyes opened. I was here again!
I shot to my feet and looked around. This time I would get some answers. But time here seemed to move much more slowly than in my reality. So I had to work fast.
I was nowhere near the valley like I was last time. There were mountains in the distance, but no civilization to be found.
I began to walk. Each step felt as though my feet were sinking into the ground below.
"Hello?" I called out, cautiously.
Last time, I remembered hearing a voice. It sounded like a man, a rather old man. He grabbed me, but then I woke up.
"Hello?" I called a bit louder, making my voice echo slightly through. The trees swayed.
"Did you call for me?"

I froze mid-step and turned around. No one was there.

That voice was the same one from before. It spoke slowly and cautiously.

"Who are you? Did you bring me here?" I called back, begging for a response.

Nothing.

"Where am I?" I cried out again.

"You know where you are, do you not?"

I breathed a sigh of relief when I heard him respond. I sat down on the grass, crossing my legs like a child.

"I'm in the cyber world, aren't I?"

Nothing.

I looked up into the dark red sky, tracing the bolts of lightning that seemed to illuminate it. "Did you bring me here?"

"...yes."

"Who are you?"

I waited for a response, but nothing came.

I tried again. "Why am I here?"

"Do not listen to him."

Him? "Who do you mean?"

I sat and listened, silently begging the voice to come back with some sort of answer.

But nothing came.

I sat up and began to walk again, the mountains in the distance becoming closer and closer.

"He will bring pain and suffering. You must not listen. He will try to keep you from me."

I paused as the voice came out again, more frantic than before. I turned around, again and again, trying to find where the voice was coming from. But to no avail.

"He will destroy everything."

"Who? Who is He?" I shouted back.

There was no response.

Salem? Is that who the voice meant? Salem will bring about the destruction of this planet, which I know and believe. It is up to me to stop him.

I know that.

I continued on in silence as the trees began to fade to black and my vision went blurry. I wanted more time, but that was out of the question.

I sat back down and waited to wake back up in my bed, back aboard The Seven Seas.

Before I regained consciousness, I heard one last thing:

"Find Xenon Tech, child."

I shielded my eyes as bright rays of sunlight assaulted me. I was back in my bed; the curtains had been drawn back. I rubbed my eyes; all signs of my late night adventure were still there. Myrah was in her normal spot, and the stains of blood were still on my pillow. Not nearly as much as last time.

I tossed my legs off the side of the bed and stretched, standing slowly. I felt fine, refreshed even. Oddly enough, nobody was here with me. Faylin wasn't here watching me, Senna wasn't checking up on me. It was almost as if...

"How much time has passed?" I raced across the room, heading for the door that connected Faylin and I.

It was unlocked.

Thankfully, he was sitting at his desk with his ever-present gray book. He barely acknowledged my presence.

"Fay, how long have I been asleep?" I asked quickly, becoming more and more nervous.

He looked up, unfazed. "Six hours and forty-seven minutes, Mr. Scarlet. Is something the matter?"

Six hours?

But, I was certain I was sleeping for longer than that. And after those strange episodes, I was always asleep for much longer.

"Are...you sure?"

He quirked his eyebrow, head tilting to the side. "Yes, Captain, we spoke only approximately seven hours ago regarding the curious case of General Myrah Flynn. Do you remember?"

Right.

After we found that it was this hybrid serum that made Myrah the way she was, we all put our files away and fell asleep. I told the team I would think about our next step overnight.

"It just feels like more time has passed. Sorry for barging in here."

Faylin sat up. "No apology needed, I was doing some research myself." He shoved a handful of the papers on his desk in the drawer.

I shut our conjoined door and walked further in Faylin's room, taking a seat in the chair across from his desk. As I looked around, I noticed his room had changed quite a bit. Most of the piles of books had been neatly organized and now filled multiple bookshelves that lined the walls. His untouched bed sat in the far corner, and his desk was situated in front of the two large and freshly-cleaned windows.

One particular item seemed to stand out though. On the edge of the bookshelf held a small green carton, no bigger than the size of my hand. I walked over to them.

"Pure Neutopian CHEM Lights."

Were these...cigarettes?

I heard some people smoked CHEM, but it was usually rather dangerous due to the obvious toxins present.

"Faylin, do you smoke?" The question sounded weird on my tongue. I felt almost like a parent, chastising their child for doing something wrong.

He looked over. "Not necessarily, I do not particularly care for it. However, an old acquaintance of mine enjoyed doing so. He gave those to me when we parted ways." He signaled me to bring him the box. "They cannot harm me in any way; I simply never saw the point."

120

He took the box into his hand and looked at it with an odd expression, thumb rubbing over the worn picture on the front. Faylin's lips tightened for a moment, as if he wanted to say something but decided against it.

The cigarette pack was opened.

I was intrigued, previous panic now gone. "Have you smoked before, Fay?"

He nodded. "I have. My acquaintance and I would do it together, often after a long night."

He looked off to the side, a seemingly happy memory passed through as the ghost of a smile appeared on his face. He tapped the box and one of the white sticks came out. He plucked it between his two fingers and tilted it back and forth to an unknown beat.

"What was their name?"

Faylin glanced at me, quirking an eyebrow. "Pardon?"

"Your acquaintance. What was their name? You seem to be close to them."

He paused, thinking for a moment before twisting the cigarette again. "We were not close, not in the way that humans are. He was simply someone I knew for a period of time. His name was Aztec."

The way Faylin said his name had an odd air to it. Something I couldn't quite comprehend. It definitely sounded like he didn't want to continue talking about him.

I smiled. "Could I try one?" It couldn't hurt me, I knew that for sure.

He looked back at me, startled for a moment. "Are you certain? They can be dangerous for your health, especially for someone of your age."

I nodded, extending my hand.

He reluctantly handed it to me, and the first thing that came to mind was how light it was. It barely weighed a thing. One side was a bluish green, and the longer side was all white. I watched as Faylin popped another one out, and fit it between his lips.

"I might as well join you, Captain."

I smiled wider and put the thing in my mouth, the same way that he did. I wasn't quite sure what to do with it though.

Faylin leaned in a bit, moving his to the corner of his mouth as he spoke. "You need to close your lips around it so it will not fall out. Hold it like this."

He manipulated my hands so I was holding it the way he was, between the index and middle finger.

"Good, now here." He reached his hand forward and grabbed the tip of my cigarette. For a moment, nothing happened, but then a quick spark ran up his hand and between his fingers, lighting the tip with a teal flame.

"Wow." I caught the stick quickly before it fell out of my mouth. I popped it in and inhaled slowly, tasting something I couldn't quite name. It was odd and nearly tasted like rainwater. Like the smell that gets trapped in your nose on a stormy day. It wasn't great, but it wasn't terrible.

Faylin leaned back in his chair and lit his own in the same fashion. The way he pulled it from his lips and blew out a stream of teal smoke looked much more elegant than the way I did, like he belonged on a billboard in the West.

I laughed, taking in another breath. Mother always ended up on those billboards. If I had to say something good about her, I could say that was she was truly something beautiful.

As beautiful as she was conniving, manipulative, and deadly.

"Mr. Scarlet." Faylin faced the window in an odd air of causality as he spoke. "This journey has taken quite an interesting turn, has it not?"

He glanced in my direction.

I hummed in response. "It has. I feel like we are running deeper and deeper down a rabbit hole right now." I blew out the smoke. "And I'm not seeing a light at the end yet."

"Yes, I agree." He went silent again. "Do you regret this? Regret digging and searching to find this to be your truth?"

"No, not at all." I knew this was the truth behind Neutopia. I knew the foul secrets that hid behind the veil of a supposed utopian society. I just didn't realize how far it had gone, just how bad it truly was.

I shook my head. "There is still something I'm missing. Something is piecing all of this together."

"An unknown element. A catalyst." He added fluidly.

I watched as the burning bits of ash vaporized into a blue mist.

"It all goes back to Xenon Tech."

END OF CHAPTER 12

13

THE LOST CHILDREN

"The Children of Galaia" Faylin cocked his head to the side as he finished his cigarette.

I figured if I wanted anyone coming close to the knowledge about Xenon Tech, and possibly the knowledge about myself, it would be Faylin. Perhaps it's because I've known him the longest, or because he's a humanoid, and so he doesn't have human irrationalities.

"Yea, apparently they were the only group that knew about the location of the Xenon Tech ruins. If it was still standing, they were the only ones who knew the location. And they were butchered for it."

"Are you sure the massacre had something to do with their knowledge of the old lab, and you are certain the old Xenon Tech Lab is the key?"

"I'm sure. For some reason, everyone who knows something about Xenon Tech dies or goes missing. The Xenon Tech scientists, The Xetyx tribe, my father and his entire team, all gone."

I don't know how Salem fits in with Xenon Tech, or even how he knew Dr. Xenon, but the timeline fits and that couldn't be a coincidence. From Discordia's records, plus my own findings, Salem arrived and began to make his way throughout society only weeks after Xenon Tech was burned to the ground. Before that, based on what father said, nobody knew him. He was nothing more than a shadow.

How would a man nobody knew be exposed to something as powerful as a nanoid? He was one of the participants that I knew for sure, but...there was a connection. I could feel it.

We remained in the North, moving northwest until we landed in Sector 1. It was exactly how Marcus said it would be; completely abandoned. Supposedly, the members of The Children of Galaia were the only ones permitted by law to live here. Either way, it worked in our favor. After the massacre, nobody dared to touch the sacred ground, and it remained abandoned.

It was past sunset when The Seven Seas landed in the middle of a forest clearing. It was beautiful, and the collection of trees made for a perfect canopy. The moon was large and bright, providing ample light and illuminating the lake in front of us. There were no birds, no animals, nothing at all. The only noise came from what I could only assume was a nearby waterfall. But there was also a quiet humming sound in the wind. It sounded like a lullaby.

I leaned forward, crossing my arms across the railing and taking in the sight. "Do you hear that humming, Faylin?

He joined me and looked towards the lake. "Luminous Tulsi."

"Luminous what?"

He pointed to one of the many bushels of flowers blooming around the lake. They were a bright blue and cast a neon glow that seemed to reflect off the water's surface. They made a pathway deeper into the forest.

"Luminous Tulsi, the Lume flower. It grows near water and can only be found in the North. It is one of the most versatile and yet puzzling forms of plant life."

Besides Lanker, who leaned by my other side, the others were still under the deck. Once they came up, I would tell them the plan.

"What makes them so confusing?" Lanker took the question right out of my mouth.

Faylin continued. "Depending on how you harvest it, and how it is ground and mixed, it can become one of two different elixirs; One being Axiom Root, a very potent and deadly toxin.

The other being Crisel Root, which is a very powerful element in medical gel and has extraordinary healing abilities. The Lume flower is considered the yin and yang of modern science."

It was truly fascinating; something so good and something so bad co-existing in one creation so perfectly. I sat up and straightened out my coat. It was freshly cleaned from my last battle, and for that I was grateful.

The door swung open and the rest of the team poured onto the deck. Everyone looked exhausted, and rightfully so. They deserved a break.

"Okay team, today's mission is simple. It'll be a nice break from the last few days."

Everyone looked relieved. Tyrinie yawned and pulled his cloak tighter like a blanket.

"Okay, what is it? What do we have to do?" His head bumped against Casteri's arm for a fraction of a second before he shook himself awake and sat up.

I pointed toward the lake. "Your job is to go down to the lake...and relax."

Everyone paused, faces painted with looks of confusion.

I smiled. "I mean it; we just finished a difficult task. I don't want y'all to be burnt out. Stretch your legs, get off the ship for a little bit, go for a swim and just relax. I'm going to handle some business of my own in the meantime."

Faylin seemed a bit shocked at this. "You are going to handle the research we spoke of on your own? Are you sure of that?"

I nodded and placed my hand on his shoulder. "You deserve a break too Faylin. Plus, I'm going to have you in charge of the crew while I'm away." He hesitated, but nodded.

"I will be back within a few hours, tops. While I'm away, no fighting, and try to only stay in this immediate area. Faylin will be in charge, so do what he says."

"Aye, Aye"

As much as it pained me to take off my coat, Faylin made a very smart observation.

Even though this sector is thought of as abandoned, there was no guarantee a patrol unit might not stroll by. It was best to keep a low profile.

So instead, I borrowed one of the Dukas family cloaks. Unlike Tyrinie's usual olive colored cloak, this one was deep silver. In addition, there was a piece that wrapped around my face, covering it from neck to nose. Only my eyes could be seen. I barely recognized myself.

An hour after leaving the landing site and finding nothing but more trees and Lume flowers, I finally began to see a break in the forest. I reached a small cliff that led down to the shoreline. It must have been far past midnight.

I took a deep breath and jumped from my grassy platform onto the sandy ground. By how it looked, it must have been some sort of sacred land for the tribe. The sand was crystal white, and large rock slabs with carvings and symbols made pathways along the beach. From here, the moon looked impossibly close and bathed the sand in an ethereal glow.

I stepped on one of the stones, following the path that it made to the sea. There seemed to be some sort of altar floating in the water. The stone walkway disappeared into the ocean, making a path at least half a mile out. The end held a large obsidian statue with hair that seemed to be made out of frosted glass.

The glass shielded their eyes and draped all the way down their body, pooling at the base, against a sunken altar pit. Large stone pillars framed both sides of the walkway, making the path feel much tighter than it actually was.

It was beautiful, though unnerving. It felt as if I wasn't supposed to be there.

I held the wrap around my face tighter, eyes squinted, as the wind began to blow. There, in the altar pit, was a person. They seemed to be kneeling, face downward.

I froze.

Who could that have been?

I squared my shoulders and slowly began walking on the stone path. With each step, the water grew deeper until it was splashing past my ankle. I looked to either side, trying to count the numerous other pillars that were scattered in the water.

I lost track after thirty-seven.

The wind blew again, disturbing the water inside the altar pit and ruffling the kneeling person's white-blonde hair. They didn't flinch, even as the wind whipped around their wet clothes.

As I stepped closer, I felt another pull. Something almost telling me to turn around and leave. I shook my head and pressed forward.

"Are you lost, stranger?"

I paused a few feet away from the kneeling person. Their voice was soft, melodic even.

"Sorry if I startled you." I responded, noting how calm they were.

"Come closer."

I took one last glance behind me before walking closer to the far end of the walkway, stepping cautiously in the altar pit. The water was a bit shallower here but it soaked my boots, making me happy I left my tights on the ship. At least my shorts weren't in danger of getting wet.

"Kneel."

I slowly crouched down before settling my knees in the cool water, sitting back on my heels. I looked to the left of me. The kneeling person was a girl, at least around my age, with light blonde hair that fell in large curls over her shoulders. She wore an outfit that looked like she was a festival dancer; tightly wrapped silk around her chest, and a long white and gold skirt that had slits that left both of her legs fully exposed. Gold cuffs surrounded her ankles, wrists, and forearms, and a golden piece of jewelry was wrapped around her head. There was gold dust around her seemingly sunken eyes and a gold line down her pallid forehead.

"Were you led here by the Matriarch?" The girl spoke slowly, eyes shut, almost as if she was in a trance. I looked back up at the obsidian statue. It loomed over me with an unsettling presence. Even though the statue's eyes couldn't be seen, I could still feel staring.

"Is that Galaia?"

The girl leaned forward into a deep bow, staying there for a moment before sitting back up.

"Do not speak the Matriarch's name so nonchalantly."

The command seemed to make the water itself shift.

I pulled the cloak closer.

"Could you tell me about Gal- I mean...the Matriarch?"

To this, the girl turned her face slightly towards me, making me grow cold. Her skin was an unhealthy shade of pale gray, and suddenly I felt as though I needed to leave.

Something didn't feel right.

"You wish to learn the teachings of the Matriarch? You tread on dangerous waters."

I nodded.

She sat up straight, face turned back towards the statue, eyes still shut. "Very well, stranger. The Xetyx people had been devoted followers of the Matriarch for many centuries. Only here, in this temple, were the teachings of the Matriarch shown. Many strangers do not wander in these parts, and only those who are pure may enter the temple." She stopped for a moment, head bowing again, almost as if she was asking permission to continue speaking. "The Purification is over, and the Great Transformation is nearing its completion."

"What's the Great Transformation?" It sounded ominous.

"According to prophecy; The Matriarch Galaia, the divine gatekeeper, would send a prophet who would destroy the old world and reshape a new world in their image. The prophet would make great changes, and rule with the iron will of the Matriarch. Once the prophet reshapes the world in the Matriarch's image, the great transformation will be complete, and the prophet will open up the barrier between this world and the 4th realm. This is truth."

"And...what will happen after this world and the, um...4th realm collide?" I've never heard of a 4th realm. Most of this didn't make sense. But there must be some sort of connection here to Xenon Tech.

She gathered two handfuls of the crystal water, holding them loosely before pouring them together into one stream. "The two worlds will become one perfect world. The Matriarch, along with her *ryn*, will emerge from the gateway and merge with the bodies of their followers, turning them into perfect and flawless beings. Those who do not follow The Matriarch will die; their bodies will not survive the merging of ryn. This is truth, and the day of The Matriarch's arrival is almost among us."

I peeked back over to her as her head craned back suddenly.

"They attempted to destroy our divine Galaia. Kill our Matriarch. They did not succeed."

A chill covered my body. That was not the voice I heard earlier. This voice was harsh and piercing, holding enough hatred in it to rival my mother.

"Heretics! The heretics will be destroyed."

Her head craned back into its normal position before she went limp in the altar, propped up on only her forearms and knees.

"Hey! Are you alrig-"

I reached out for her, but before I could make contact with her, a surge of energy seemed to flow through her, pushing me back.

When I opened my eyes, I was back on the beach, staring up at
the moon overhead.

What the hell was that...?
While I was tempted to rush back to the ship, I noticed another
clearing down the far side of the beach. It was illuminated by
more Lume flowers and seemed to lead deeper into the forest.
I hesitated.
The only reason I came out here was to find the temple and more
information about Xenon Tech, it would be a complete waste of
time to go back empty-handed. At least that's what I tried to
convince myself.
When I looked back, the girl in the altar pit seemed to have
vanished, but Galaia's statue still seemed to bore into me. I
shivered and began to walk.
The trail was lit by nothing but Lume flowers; the further I went
the more they seemed to appear. There were stone archways that
passed overhead every few minutes. It was truly something
beautiful.
I kept my cloak pulled tight as the wind began to blow violently.
The air itself seemed to be alive, and the feeling was unnerving
me more than I could comprehend.
More than that, the dark was something that I never liked, and
this darkness just seemed suffocating.
Father would often berate me for my hatred of the dark.
Before long, I found myself out of the forest and into a clearing.
It was beyond anything I had ever seen, especially in the Western
Region.
It seemed to resemble the ruins of an ancient temple from the old
world. There was a waterfall that seemed to have been hundreds
of feet tall, surrounding the area on three sides and feeding into a
grand lake that went beneath the stone bridge I stood on and far
into the woods. Numerous pillars, some standing tall and others
worn from age, scattered throughout the lake, wrapped in

hundreds of Lume plants. At the base of the waterfall stood the entrance of the stone temple. It was a large platform with jagged walls that arched upwards like a cathedral, but with no windows or ceiling. It must have been centuries old.

"This is it, it has to be."

I nodded to myself as I started to walk forward, glancing around me quickly. This place was abandoned, no doubt. So why did I feel as though I was being watched?

The air became thick with mist after reaching the platform. Another door appeared and it looked almost as if it led into the waterfall itself. I placed both hands on two of the doors largest circles, an eerie red ring appear around both of them. The door opened with a groan and closed silently once I entered.

For a moment, everything was dark. Moonlight began to fill the corridor I was in, and the Lume plants along the wall hummed and glowed. There were twin streams of water cascading down either side of the hall.

"It's beautiful here." Along the walls were more intricate symbols and pictures, many of which I couldn't understand.

"The temple is lovely, yes."

I jumped, fists ready, as I came face to face with none other than R.

"Damn it, R! I knew I was being followed. Would it kill you to announce you're here before giving me a heart attack?" My voice seemed to echo over the deafening roar of the waterfalls, R simply looked amused.

"Well I could, but where would the fun in that be?"

R seemed to be back to his normal self.

I shook my head, looking closer at the wall carvings. While some seemed to tell a story, some images stood on their own, surrounded by more symbols. Most of the creatures look a bit like how they portrayed this Galaia person; inhumanly long and lean with hair that faded into transparency encasing most of their body. They almost looked human in appearance, but their bodies seemed to be covered in circles and lines.

"Either way, it's nice of you to finally show up." My hands brushed over the carvings, wiping off some of the moss that had grown. "You know, I could have used your help earlier on the beach."

He yawned and leaned back, scratching his ear with his pinky. "Nah, it looked like you had everything taken care of. It wears me out to keep appearing to you, I only do it when I need to." He looked over at me with a smirk on his face. "Plus, to be completely honest, I can't stand this place."

"Why?"

He simply shrugged, so I continued on.

"What are those creatures surrounding the Matriarch?"

R paused, looking at where I was pointing. "Those are *ryn*; divine creatures that inhabit the 4th realm. They're servants to The Matriarch. When did you suddenly become interested in mythology?"

I nodded. "I didn't actually expect you to know the answer. Since when were you an expert on the Xetyx Tribe?"

R chuckled and pointed at his head. "Um, Nanoid, remember?"

Right. If it exists anywhere in cyberspace, R already knows it.

END OF CHAPTER 15

14

THE GLASS ROOM

W e reached the end of the hall as another door appeared. I opened it in the same fashion as the previous door. This room seemed to have been some sort of common room for all of the tribe members. It was huge, so much so that I was certain the Seven Seas would be able to fit comfortably in here. The ceiling had horizontal slits that went the length of the room and surrounded a large, circular, transparent glass pane. Strange orbs, seemingly made of water, floated throughout the air, sending beams of blue light cascading in different directions. The room was bathed in a blue glow, which seemed to bounce off of the water covered floor. The streams of water from the hallway pooled into this room – there was at least a foot or so of water that we waded through. More Lume flowers scattered around the ground, some under the water and some peeking through. But the majority of them seemed to congregate around the center of the room, surrounding another statue. This one, like the one on the beach, was made out of pure obsidian. The statue was sitting, back straight, and head thrown back. Their legs were crossed tightly, and their arms crossed their chest, palms facing the ceiling. Each hand held a large orb; one that seemed to have black gas gathering inside, and the other with a red gas. The hair started off as a white frosted glass but became transparent as it flowed down their body.

This one was at least twice the size of the first, and sat upon an impressive pedestal that was covered in more markings.

We walked further into the room, the water being noticeably colder than it was in the hall. R pointed towards the statue.

"That's the Matriarch. The old tribe believed that this statue provided balance and order to the temple, and to the people inside. We see how well that went over."

"Sad, isn't it. Why would someone kill off this entire tribe? All of these people, children, everyone. It doesn't make any sense." All of this, just to hide the Xenon Tech lab.

I followed R down one of the many doors that lined the walls.

"Humankind doesn't make sense. It never has, and probably never will. They don't need a reason to kill one another, and honestly, even if E didn't step in, humanity would have destroyed itself sooner or later."

"Well, that's rather pessimistic."

"I hate to tell you this, kid, but whether you believe it or not, humanity is obsolete. I don't know if this world is even really worth saving." R glanced over at me, quiet for a moment before breaking out into a smile. "I mean, this is your mission, you do whatever you want. Daddy knows better than I do. I'm just a nanoid."

He laughed in his normal boisterous tone. I tuned him out.

The hall led us to a corridor with many doors on both sides. I could imagine the faint sound of snoring coming from many of them. We stopped at a door that was slightly ajar; the door itself had the symbol of a circle with a dot in the center.

Curiosity got the best of me as I pushed it open.

The room was rather small but had two simple beds on both far walls. More of the floating orbs drifted across the ceiling, and Lume flowers hung like lanterns, filling the room with a light hum.

I shrugged, fiddling with my ear cuff, turning it on.

"Scarlet to Faylin, can you hear me?" I whispered. The cuff crackled slightly, but no sound came out. The line was dead. I tried again, but this time, not even crackling came out. Surely the team was fine.

"Sorry kid, but we are pretty far underground. I don't think that's gonna work down here."

We began to walk further up another set of stairs and across more halls. I lost track of time.

"R, any idea where the archives will be?" He knew so much about these people, I figured it was a normal question.

However, no answer came. I spared a glance back, R was gone. I shivered again, pulling the cloak closer.

I shielded my eyes as bright lights came forth, the smell of wet grass was heavy. I started slowly down the hallway, brushing my damp hair out of my face. The large hall seemed to act as a greenhouse, as Lume flowers, in all different colors, filled the space nearly to capacity. The room was steamy, too steamy, and I dreaded keeping the cloak wrapped around my face. I looked up, trying to find the source of light and heat. The orbs had changed colors; instead of being a clear blue like before, they were a bright yellow, creating the look, and apparently the feel, of sunlight.

My feet splashed faster through the cool water that flooded the room nearly to my calf, reaching the door on the opposite side. Some of the orbs hovered closer to the ground. I knelt, curiously poking at one softly, making the water shift.

It was warm, as I had imagined.

I had seen a lot of technology in my life, but this was completely new. There was no CHEM source, so whatever was making them do this was a mystery.

I cupped it into my hand fully. As soon as I did, the water began to shift and skew.

I rotated my hand around the base of the orb, trying to keep it in place. I closed my eyes, breathing deeply and focusing, bringing just the slightest bit of red along my hands.

The orb stilled, and the water inside began to spin.

I laughed, staring transfixed.

I wished the others could've seen it!

For a moment, it looked just like the others that were floating along the ceiling.

A spark of red zipped through the water, making the spinning stop. Soon the outside of the orb shifted and became covered in red streaks. In a loud burst, the orb exploded, covering me completely in water.

"Well, I guess it couldn't have been that simple." I chuckled, wiping the red-tinted water off my face as I continued along my way.

For the third time that day, I came face to face with a large stone door adorned with numerous circles on it. I looked around one last time before placing both hands on the door. The circles began to glow red before the door slowly shifted open.

I was greeted by an impossibly large circular room. The walls were made completely out of intricate glass panes that weaved their way to the ceiling, and large orbs floated aimlessly. The entire bottom level of the room was filled with crystal water. There was a stone bridge that led over to a large platform that held a spiral staircase.

I cautiously stepped forward before zipping my way across. The staircase seemed to be made of some sort of white gem. It shone brilliantly and seemed to reflect every color in the room.

The second level held large bookcases that were lined against the back windows, framed in moss and Lume flowers. Numerous tables and stands, filled with papers, scattered throughout the room. It seemed as though this was a study or an office.

I felt a presence. "Is anyone here?" I whispered as I made my way to one of the tables, looking around cautiously.

"Just me, kid."

I whipped my head around to find *R* sitting on the ledge of the platform.

"Thank you for finally showing up again. Where did you go?" I rushed over and sat next to him, overlooking the door where I just entered.

He yawned again, stretching out on the table. "I told you, kid. It wears me out to stay like this for too long. See?" He held up his arm, shaking it lightly. Little bits of code seemed to shed off like dust, disappearing into vapor. "And honestly, it's not that good for you either. I'm causing a strain on your head by doing this. Trust me, this is all for *your* benefit, my little vessel."

I felt my cheeks go red in irritation. "Eh, don't use me as an excuse for you being lazy, a little bit of strain isn't going to kill anyone."

I stood up in a huff, mentally berating myself for sounding like Tyrinie.

"Well, are you going to sit there, or are you going to help me?" R stood, muttering something under his breath. "Alright captain-y, what are we looking for?"

"Anything that has to do with Xenon Tech." I paused for a moment. "Actually, look for anything having to do with the Xetyx people as well."

"Ah, looks like you're diving right into the heart of it. My little host is really growing up."

I ignored him and began looking up and down one of the bookshelves.

Many were various volumes of "The Matriarch's Teachings" and "Indigenous Northern Plant Life".

I peeked over my shoulder and spotted R sitting on one of the tables, looking through a book that seemed to be filled with pictures.

"Hmm...Say, kid, did you know E is my twin?"

My hand froze, hovering over the fifteenth volume of a book on Lume flowers.

"What? E, as in the nanoid in Salem?"

"Yup, well, not in the human sense of having the same parents. Rather, we were created at the same time. We even look alike."

I continued to look through the next shelf – this one covered plant life before in the old world. I was getting closer.

"Wait, so E has red hair as well?"

R chuckled. "No no, do you really think I naturally look like this? My projected image is mostly because of your mind's influence, and your DNA's influence. Truth is, if you were to ever see me in cyberspace, you wouldn't recognize me. When we are in our natural state, it is difficult for the untrained eye to distinguish nanoids from one another, especially E and myself."

"So why do I have red hair and eyes? I thought that that was because of you?"

R shrugged his shoulders. "Eh, side effects…"

I rolled my eyes and stayed quiet as R spoke again, flipping through the book. "You see, nanoids aren't born, not in the human sense anyway. We are created for a certain purpose. I have been with E for most of my existence, well minus the past few hundred years. I haven't seen E in so long, it's odd."

I suppressed a groan. "What's odd?"

As much as I wanted to hear more of R's story, he was making it nearly impossible to concentrate.

"That E hasn't appeared to me, hasn't tried to contact me."

I shrugged, passing over a book on sunflowers. "Maybe he's mad at you, I mean, you are technically working with the person who is trying to kill him." I replied absentmindedly as I went to the next shelf.

"Kill him, or kill his vessel?"

I stopped as I found a written collection of pre-war events. "What do you mean by that?"

140

"Just what I said. Aren't you going after Salem? If so, then E shouldn't be your target."

"...E and Salem are one and the same." I flipped through the first few pages, finding dates as far back as the 2450's. "Geez, this book is ancient."

"What like how you and I are one and the same? Are we the same person?"

"So, you're saying that E is a completely different entity? That I should somehow kill Salem, but not the nanoid in him? What even happens to a nanoid once their vessel is killed?"

R shrugged and finished flipping through the book. "Hell if I know. Don't mind me, kid, I'm just talking to fill the silence."

"I never actually thought of things that way, but...we need to stay focused. The sooner we find the connection to Xenon Tech, the sooner we can find more about the nanoids and the Hybrid Theory. Then after we shut that down, we can take out Salem and all of his followers." I pulled out a book with a picture of a pre-war Neutopia on the cover. "After Salem is out of the picture, I will break all of these other mysteries apart."

I ran my finger across the image on the cover. "R, what was Neutopia called before the Salem changed everything?"

"It was called Earth."

I nodded.

I opened the front cover – tiny cursive was scribbled on the inside. I squinted to read it:

Brother,

The structures listed above are the ones you requested. Every single one survived the prophet's planetary transformation. The Gateway, as we predicted, was unharmed – along with the remains of the Lab. Each piece holds vital information for the coming of our Matriarch. The artifacts that could be moved were sent to the same resting place as the Lab and the observatory.

Farhill Valley will remain uninhabited – holding the ruins of the past. I have sent word to our Lord Salem, and he has agreed to keep it under the protection of the Xetyx people. This is now your burden.

Hold fast and Godspeed.

I tilted my head and reread the note.
This was it.
This was what I needed.
The Lab they mentioned must have been Xenon Tech Labs. They said it, along with the other ruins, were being held in Farhill Valley.
I had never heard of such a place.
"I got it R, I think I found the information I need." I held the book close to my chest and stood, working out the kinks in my back.
"R, did you hear me?"
I froze.
A light groan began to fill the air, but I didn't recognize that voice. The sound came from the doorway on the bottom level.
Footsteps began coming towards the staircase.
I took a peek over the railing.
It was the girl from earlier, on the beach. Her soaked white garb slid lazily across the floor, sticking to her gray legs. Her eyes, still unfocused and blank, were searching the room.
I jumped and tucked the book into my cloak, sliding under one of the tables, sitting perfectly still.
The wet footsteps slowed down and began to creep up the staircase. I closed my eyes and focused on the clearing outside of the forest where my team was. There was still so much to explore, but my time was up.

In a burst of red, I was sitting back in the middle of the dark woods – a few water orbs floated around me. They must've tagged along.

I breathed out in relief.

I pulled out the large book. It looked like I had a lot of reading to get done.

By the time I reached the landing spot, it must've been nearly 2 or 3 am. Everyone seemed to be back on the ship, except for one. Faylin sat by the water, surrounded by notes and papers. He seemed to be fixated on them, looking through them rapidly. He was so deep in thought, he didn't notice my presence. There was something unnerving about the scene in front of me.

Faylin, who was usually so level-headed and calm, seemed bothered. Something was off.

"...Faylin. What are you doing?"

His head popped up, papers scattered in the light wind. He caught them with minimum effort.

"Captain, you are back early, are you not?"

He pulled the papers in tightly, still not meeting my eye.

"Yea, I found what I was looking for. It took me longer than I expected, but I tried to make it back quickly." I pulled the book out from my cloak. He didn't seem to notice.

I went over to the water's edge, taking a seat next to Faylin.

He pulled the papers in tighter.

"Fay, what's going on? Is everything alright?"

He glanced over at me, pausing before finally pulling the papers away from his chest. I looked over at them.

They were notes, letters, and files, all with the same name.

"Dr. Cyryl Plaski. You're doing some more research on him?"

He nodded.

I let out a relieved sigh. "Well, why did you need to hide that? There's no problem with doing extra research. Even though I did tell you all to relax for the evening, I'll forgive you this time for not listening."

I smiled and looked back over to Faylin. Oddly enough, he didn't respond, and his face looked just as stern and troubled as it did before.

"Captain...something else is troubling me."

He handed me a stack of the papers. I looked at the picture of the doctor. There was something oddly familiar about him.

He looked to be in his forties; pale skin, framed by silvery gray hair that nearly matched his eyes perfectly. He wore a stern expression and a stark white lab coat.

Where have I seen this man before?

"This man, Dr. Plaski, is my creator."

The air seemed to freeze at that moment.

END OF CHAPTER 14

15

AWAKENING

I waited with a heavy presence for Faylin to continue to speak.

But no words came.

He just continued to stare at the image in his hand.

Looking closer now, I could see the resemblance; Faylin must've truly been made in Dr. Plaski's image.

They shared the same silvery hair, the same fairness of skin, the same gray eyes, and in certain situations, even the same expression. If it wasn't for the fact Faylin was created, I would say he truly looked like he could've been Dr. Plaski's actual son.

"Are you certain? Is he really your creator?"

It was a stupid question I felt I already knew the answer to. But I needed to hear it again.

He nodded absentmindedly.

"That is my Master. I could never forget his face. Even though...it has been so long since I have seen him."

That's right. From what Faylin told me when we first met, his "Master" abandoned him. Vanished into thin air, leaving Faylin behind. I suppose that makes sense; he ran off to rejoin Salem. But then...why create Faylin in the first place?

I was jarred from my thoughts when Faylin began gathering the papers, standing up quietly.

"My apologies Captain, I will be retiring to my room early tonight."

He headed off to the ship without another word.

"Captain, please report to the deck. Thank you."

I placed my unfinished letter to Persephone down as the command spoke out. I stood and grabbed my coat, stretching before heading out of the door.

The past two days had been rather quiet. Too quiet. After the conversation I had with Faylin, he went to his room and hadn't been out. I, along with some of the crew, had all taken turns knocking and trying to coax him out. But to no avail.

Everyone was convinced Faylin and I had some argument, which I was fine with them believing. It was not my place to spread around what Faylin had told me, besides; I didn't need any hostility on board.

I walked past Faylin's room. It was as silent as it had been for the past two days. I gave a pitiful knock.

Still no answer.

I turned the doorknob.

It was still locked.

I sighed and kept walking. Of course, I could've just teleported into his room, but there was no way I could have explained that to him. Plus, it would have been a complete invasion of privacy. If Faylin needed time to himself to figure things out, I should give it to him.

The sun was high in the sky as we passed over the ocean between the North and the West Region. Dr. Cyryl Plaski, along with his serums of destruction, was our target. As long as Dr. Plaski still had his lab and his "Hybrid Mother" serum, Salem could continue replacing every member of The Management I took down. His production had to be stopped.

"It's about time you showed up! Have you made nice with Faylin yet? I'm so tired of eating Lanker's cooking."

Tyrinie crossed his arms and huffed under his cloak. I rolled my eyes at his complaining.

"No Tyrinie, Faylin is still in his room. And if you are so tired of Lanker's cooking, why don't you cook for yourself. You have two paws that aren't broken."

I smirked as his nostrils flared in anger.

Before I could speak, Casteri popped over and placed his hand on Tyrinie's head. "That's enough Tyrinie, leave the Captain alone." Beside him was a magnificent piece. Obviously the finished product of whatever he was working on days before. A large and sleek silver hover-cycle; finished with red glass veins and our ship's emblem. It was beautiful.

"Captain, meet T-34, our new virtually intelligent infiltration vehicle. Given the fact that the Eastern Region is majority desert, this would be the smarter way to travel, as opposed to traveling via ship and possibly being detected."

Casteri gave the device a slight tap, and it glided over to me, stopping when it bumped against my leg.

He chuckled, "Go ahead and give it a try, I have three made currently. Thanks to Marcus, I was able to make them fairly quickly."

"This is amazing work Casteri, I'm embarrassed to say it, but I've never actually ridden something like this before."

I gripped both of the handles; it bobbed up and down as if it were in water. I took a deep breath and lifted one leg, wrapping it around the underside before taking a hesitant seat.

The stability lasted for only a moment before it jerked to the side, and I was upside down.

I squeaked in surprise before my grip loosened, and I crashed onto the ship.

There was a moment of silence before Tyrinie burst out into laughter.

"Very graceful, I couldn't have done it better myself!"

I glared in embarrassment as I stood and dusted myself off. Casteri and Marcus looked rather amused but spared me the mockery.

"Enjoy the laughter Tyrinie, this will be no problem." I pushed my hair back, before repeating the same motion, stepping on the T-34 slowly...

...before ending up upside down again.

Though this time was even less graceful than the other, as I was completely thrown a few feet to the left.

Tyrinie rolled on the floor in fits of laughter, nearly losing his cape in the process. Marcus rushed over and grabbed me by the elbow, hoisting me up.

"You almost had it little man; it's like riding a bike. But try not to go one leg at a time, you'll lose your balance that way. Just push 'er down, and hop on. Watch me."

Marcus held the handles as I did before jumping up and mounting the T-34 in one smooth motion.

"See, it's easy, no stress!"

Easy for him to say.

I gave a forced chuckle as Marcus exited, urging me forward.

"Of course...easy...no stress."

C'mon Scarlet, this should be no problem for you. It's not like I haven't done more difficult feats.

I took a deep breath, holding the handles down, and swinging myself on the bike like how Marcus did. As soon as I was seated, I felt the same jolt before the entire cycle veered backwards, throwing me off.

Before I could brace for impact, I felt myself being caught by an even more solid grip.

"Mr. Scarlet, please be careful before you injure yourself."

I smiled at the familiar voice before setting myself upright. "Nice to see you too, Fay."

Before he could respond, the rest of the crew ran over and greeted him, demanding answers of what had happened between us.

Faylin seemed taken aback by all of the attention, before glancing over at me.

"Please excuse my temporary absence. There was an urgent matter I needed to attend to, and I could not have been bothered. The Captain did nothing wrong. But, I do appreciate the concern."

Marcus leaned over and placed Faylin in a headlock, ruffling his hair. "Fifi, you had all of us worried! Next time you have urgent matters, or whatever, handle it in the lab so we know you're alive! Plus, we were all about to beat up the Captain if he did something."

I rolled my eyes and laughed.

Nice to know I was the prime suspect.

Everything felt as though it was back to normal; Lanker and Tyrinie stayed above deck on lookout duty, Casteri was in his lab working on more of his T-34 projects, Senna offered to take care of dinner, while Faylin, Marcus, and I huddled in Faylin's lab. Apparently, Marcus was one of the only people Faylin trusted to know his secret. Something about Marcus having one of the most leveled heads, and in my opinion, one of the biggest hearts.

We all sat around the table, going through papers and files. Faylin was so focused he didn't respond to either of us.

"So this is the guy, huh? Dr. Cyryl Plaski. I gotta say I see the resemblance, which is really odd." Marcus held the picture of Cyryl up to Faylin's face.

I yawned, rubbing the sleep from my eyes. "Why is that an odd thing?"

"Well..." Marcus continued, plopping in his chair. "Most humanoids are made in an overly idealistic image, a perfect image. Not too often do you see one made in a familial image. For example, an artist would make a humanoid that looked extraordinarily artistic, perhaps with different colored eyes or exotic hair and skin.

While a historian would have a humanoid that looked as if they just walked out of an 18th century French soiree. Usually, you never make a humanoid in your image unless...you're trying to replace someone."

Marcus paused again before pulling through some more files. "Did Dr. Cyryl have a child?"

A child?

I looked over to Faylin, who seemed to ponder the question himself.

"I...believe as much. I am not certain though, I apologize. My memory, oddly enough, is quite fuzzy from back then. I only remember pieces."

"You can't remember? Seriously? I don't think I've ever heard of a humanoid that forgot something." Marcus laughed lightheartedly. "We'll keep looking."

"Well, it looks like we have another man way out of his time." Marcus jarred me awake, shoving a hologram in my face. "I was wondering why I couldn't find any information about Cyryl; I forgot I was looking in the wrong century. Look at this."

The database Marcus pulled up didn't seem to be from the census. The site itself seemed to be from some underground net. Sure enough, the information on Cyryl seemed legitimate.

I scrolled through his pictures; most of them were of him in a lab coat, standing sternly in front of different lab equipment, working with a team of unrecognizable people.

Marcus pulled the database away from me while typing in some more code. "Look who else I found." The page loaded up, and another image appeared, a young woman with stark white hair and impossibly gray eyes. "Looks like we found your template. This beauty's name was Nilya Plaski, Dr. Plaski's daughter and only child. She died rather young- age nineteen, from cardiac arrest."

"She died from a heart attack as a teenager?"

"Sounds odd, right? There might be something there to look into, but one thing is for certain." Marcus pulled up the blown picture of Nilya's face, holding it next to Faylin. "He definitely modeled you after her."

The resemblance was more than uncanny, it was a mirror image. Marcus shrugged, "I guess, in some way, this was your sister." Faylin held the image for a moment before placing it down. "This does not answer any questions though. Perhaps there were things that she knew about the experiments or the hybrid mother, but there is no way to ask her now."

Marcus gave a light laugh. "Well, there's a good chance she didn't know anything anyway."

"Why is that?" I questioned.

"Well think about it, this guy might be twisted, but it looked like he made Faylin to fill the hole in his heart after his child died. It looked like his wife died during childbirth, and Nilya is all that he had. If he cared enough about her to basically make an immortal version of her, he must've cared for her dearly. He wouldn't have put her in danger or exposed her to any of this. At least that's what I think."

"Well," I stood up and stretched. "It looks like we can just ask Cyryl ourselves when we meet him. Let's get some rest. Tomorrow is going to be a busy day."

"You don't have to tell me twice. G'night, little man." Marcus got up before bouncing out the room quickly.

Faylin didn't move, he just continued to look over more and more information, staring intently at Cyryl's image as if he was waiting for it to move.

"Faylin?"

No response.

I walked over, shaking his shoulder. "That means you too, go to bed and get some rest."

He nodded absentmindedly.

"Of course, Mr. Scarlet. I will in just one moment."

"I mean it, I better not find you here when I wake up."

I made a beeline for my room, rest sounded more than tempting. However, I actually wanted R to show up. But of course, whenever I want him around, he never shows up.

A light tap on my shoulder woke me from my sleep.

I grunted and shoved the hand away, burying my face back in my pillow. The tap returned more forcefully this time.

"Mr. Scarlet, please wake up."

I groaned. "Fay? Is everything alright?"

I sat up, brushing my hair back in an attempt to tame it.

"Yes, I simply have a question for you. A request, if you will."

"And...this couldn't wait until the morning?" I peeked at my clock, it blinked 4:37 am.

"I am afraid not, I needed to bring this to you now. Can you please join me in my room when you are ready?"

Faylin's face was stern and steady, per usual. But something felt off about the exchange. For the millionth time, I wished that I could read what on earth he was thinking.

"Yea, of course."

Faylin nodded and left the room swiftly. I yawned, cracking my neck and arms before tossing on my clothes from the night before.

Something told me I wouldn't be going back to bed after this.

It wasn't more than ten minutes before I was knocking on Faylin's door. There was a quiet shuffle from inside before the door opened.

Faylin donned his normal uniform, minus his coat. His hair was pulled back and neatly braided in a way that I had never seen before.

"Captain, please come in."

Faylin stepped aside and allowed me to enter. The room looked the same from a few days ago, same bookshelves, same papers, and same half-full carton of cigarettes.

Faylin stopped in front of his desk, watching me closely as I sat in the chair in front of him.

"What's going on Faylin? Is everything alright?" I leaned back, trying to make myself comfortable with those silver eyes monitoring my every movement.

"Mr. Scarlet, how much do you know about humanoids and humanoid ownership?"

Humanoid...ownership?

Truth be told, I never knew much about humanoids in general. Father never trusted them and encouraged me not to either. He said they were unnatural, a false hope given to human society in a moment of weakness. The fact I trusted Faylin was the biggest "risk" in my life. I guess Faylin just seemed different, so he seemed safe.

But in all, I never knew how they were owned. I just assumed they were programmed a certain way after they were bought.

"Nothing to be honest"

He took a breath before standing up even straighter. "When a humanoid is first created, some of the human owner's DNA is implanted into their system, in essence, rewriting them. It creates a permanent link between the humanoid itself and the unique strands of DNA within the human master. Usually, this is done right as the humanoid is activated. However, this is not the only time this act can be done."

Faylin trailed off, quirking his eyebrow as if to ask whether or not I understood.

I nodded quickly. "Okay, I'm following you."

To be honest, he completely lost me.

Faylin continued, taking a deep breath. "Sometimes, an *unofficial* bond between a humanoid and a potential master can be done.

This is usually for instances where a humanoid is sold illegally, stolen, or sold after their previous master died or gave them up. This bond still involves the potential master's DNA, but it is done differently because the humanoid is already activated. It is not painful, and causes no harm to either party."

Faylin paused again, but this time I spoke up.

"Sorry Fay, I really don't follow you. What does reprogramming humanoids have to do with anything? Why are you telling me this? And, what's this unofficial bond you mentioned?"

Faylin sighed and walked towards me, stopping only a few feet away. He then lowered himself to the ground, resting on his knees. He straightened his back, sitting prim and proper as always.

"I am asking something of you, making you a bargain. And I would like to ask you to follow through with it."

I focused on Faylin's face as he focused his eyes on me.

"Mr. Scarlet, I am asking you to take full ownership over me. I am giving you the option to perform the unofficial bond and have me belong solely to you."

I froze; it felt as if time itself had stopped. I swallowed dryly. Faylin continued as if he sensed my hesitation.

"This would be extraordinarily beneficial to you, Mr. Scarlet. Once you own me, if you agree to it, you would be able to command me as you please. There will be no questioning or resistance to what you say. I could never question your cause, nor could I question anything you might have me do under your command. You would never have to worry about me abandoning your cause. I would be everything you need and more. This would be of great help to you."

Faylin still stared at me with that steely, unbreakable gaze.

I was speechless. He wanted to give me his freedom. He wanted me to turn him into a tool, into my tool. The thought made my stomach churn as a sense of familiarity began to settle.

Nothing but a weapon

"Please, Captain," The sudden break from silence sent a shiver up my spine. "I would like you to do this. This would benefit both of us greatly."

No, this wouldn't *benefit* him. He shouldn't want this from me. "Is that...really something you would want Faylin? You would really want to give up your freedom? Just like that?"

He paused before nodding slowly and reaching out for my arm. He flipped my hand over, exposing my bare wrist, pointing a painted nail to my vein.

"Blood is the easiest way. Just a small sample, no more than two vials. One would need to be injected into three specific areas of my brain; Casteri or Marcus could assist with the operation. The other vial would need to be mixed with CHEM and ingested. Once it is absorbed into my body, it will complete the rewriting process. It would not cause you any pain, and the process would not take more than an hour.

"But, why? Why me? Why now? Is there something that you aren't telling me? Are you having doubts about the mission?"

"No, Mr. Scarlet, quite the opposite." Faylin sat up a tad bit more, still holding my wrist. "I believe in you and in your mission. I want to follow you. But this new discovery changes things."

"With Dr. Cyryl?"

Faylin nodded.

"All of these years, I assumed my master was dead. And because there was nobody to inherit me, I was left master-less. There was no other human I truly followed or obeyed until you found me. But now we know not only is my master alive, but he is working for our enemy. That fact puts us at a huge disadvantage. I still belong to Dr. Plaski, and when he finds I am with you, all he would need to do is command me...and I would be forced to listen. Almost as if a switch would go off in my brain. I could be made to fight against you Captain, or worse."

His grip on me tightened. "But you could override that if you choose to complete the bond and own me. At that point, his ownership would be voided. I would belong to you alone."

I stared back at Faylin, completely frozen, trying to comprehend what I had just heard. Faylin was begging me to set him free from Cyryl, but the only way to do that would be to put my own leash on him.

The thought sickened me.

Faylin was his own person, and one of the few people I considered not only a crewmate, but a friend. If I knew Faylin was only by my side, forced to kill those I chose, only because he had no other choice, I wouldn't be able to live with myself. It made me feel like I was stripping him of his free will, forcing him into slavery.

But he doesn't have free will. Humanoids don't have free will.

I heard R clear as a bell.

This could be just what you need. An advantage. A humanoid at your beck and call. It would be perfect.

Faylin always did as I asked, but he never had a problem giving his opinion. Was that simply because he wasn't "owned". Was my perception of his freedom simply Faylin drifting down an unnatural and unsafe path. Could he actually be free?

Maybe this was simply the only way I could help him.

Just do it, kid. Give him your blood and bind him to you.

Faylin looked down for a moment. "Mr. Scarlet, I...do not wish to be under the command Dr. Plaski. Not again."

Faylin had told Marcus and me that he didn't remember much from his past. But with the way he said that, there was definitely more. There was something he wasn't telling me.

My mouth was dry, and my stomach felt ill. If this was what Faylin wanted, how could I say no? And maybe this could be what I needed.

This was the only way that I could help him.

I felt calmer when I remembered my mission and my father. That was all that truly mattered.

This ship and this crew were what I needed to make this mission happen, I couldn't let feelings cloud my purpose.

The calm feeling turned into numbness as I distanced myself from what I was about to do.

I opened my mouth.

"I can't."

My eyes shot open. The words came out before I could stop them.

Faylin cocked his head, shock covering his face as well. "What?"

It was the most human I had ever heard him sound.

I tried to reel my emotions back in, tried to fill my head with the numbing thoughts of my father and my mission.

But I couldn't.

"I can't do that to you Faylin, you're my friend. My...actual friend. I can't just bind you to me and force you to be here. I-I want you to be here because it's what *you* want to do. I want you to tell me when something I'm doing is stupid. I want you to give me your opinion! I don't want a pawn or a tool, I want you here the way you are."

Faylin seemed to be at a loss of words.

"But Mr. Scarlet, when my master-"

"Who cares about Cyryl or any of the Management in that case? Faylin, I might not know much about humanoids, I mean, hell, I barely know anything about you. But I do know this. I do know you are different. And I believe you can take whatever Cyryl might try to throw at you. I think you are strong enough to handle that. You are unlike any humanoid I have ever seen, and I can't just own you."

I pulled my hand from Faylin's loosened grip, causing his hand to fall silently back in his lap.

I sighed, hesitantly placing my hand on his head. "I'm sorry Fay. I can't even begin to start to explain how humbled I am to know you would want me, of all people, in such an important role. I could think of plenty of others that would be more than qualified. But, I don't want to own you. I just want you to be here…as my friend, and my first mate. Is that okay?"

Faylin paused before sighing before rolling back on his heels and standing in one smooth motion. He held his hand out to me.

"Well, I cannot force you to complete the bond, and if that is what you truly want, I will respect it. However, I cannot say I fully understand your reasoning."

I grabbed his hand, hoisting myself up.

"Do you not understand me wanting you to be my friend?"

"That much I do understand. I do not understand why you would not want to give yourself that advantage over my master. As of now, you have more than just Dr. Plaski to worry about. There is also the possibility that I might-"

"I'm not worried about Cyryl, and I'm not going to give myself an advantage that includes ripping your free will from you. I don't care what anyone else says, in my eyes, you are your own person. And I intend on keeping it that way."

We walked out of the doorway and headed onto the main deck, all thoughts of sleep had vanished from my mind.

"I never have, and never will see you as my tool or my weapon. You will be fine against Cyryl. And after we're finished with him, you won't have to worry about anything, and you really will be free. Is that clear?"

Faylin nodded, pushing the hair out of his face.

"Of course, Captain."

END OF CHAPTER 15

16

A NEW ALLY

The sun was high in the sky when the others emerged from their respected cabins. Lanker and Tyrinie were by the helm, per usual. Casteri and Marcus were each in their labs; Marcus working on Faylin's dilemma with Cyryl, and Casteri working on making my T-34 a bit more "beginner-friendly". Senna insisted on dragging me into his lab again to clean some of the wounds on my hands, only to be surprised that they had healed already.
I didn't bother mentioning the new ones.

Meanwhile, Faylin and I were in my office, overlooking the foggy ocean. Only a few hours away from the Eastern Region. Faylin was quiet, quieter than usual. I assumed he was still concerned over coming face-to-face with his master.
I could understand the fear.
There were still so many things about his past I didn't understand. Why did Dr. Cyryl suddenly up and leave him? He went through all of the trouble of making Faylin look identical to his daughter, only to leave. It made no sense. And it seemed so strange that a humanoid as unique, beautiful, and obviously as high tech as Faylin would remain master-less for so long. Why did nobody try to bond with him?
And then, Faylin's face when he said he didn't want to be forced to go back to Cyryl. What was all that about?

So many unanswered questions, but this didn't seem like the proper time to ask.

Before I could say anything, a frantic knock came at the door. Lanker rushed in, slamming the door against the wall in the process. "Captain, we need you on the deck!"

"Is everything okay?" I grabbed my coat, straightened it while following him.

"Looks like we have some company."

I shielded my eyes against the bright mid-afternoon sun as a ship approached from the distance. It was inky black with gold and red accents staining the sides. The flag was black, adorned with an opened mouth skull that had dirty rusted nails sticking through every side of its head.

I felt calm, nervous, and a bit tense all at the same time. I recognized that flag all too well.

"Calm down everyone, we aren't in danger." I sighed. "Just, don't say anything. Let me talk."

Everyone looked at me in shock, lowering their weapons.

"Are you sure Captain? They don't look too friendly." Lanker looked a bit skeptical as the ship approached even faster, lowering their bridge to the level of our deck.

"Trust me, I can handle this one."

I squared my shoulders and fixed my coat, giving a bright smile as their Captain came into view.

The bridge connected, and as soon as it stabilized, three sets of boots made their way across and onto my deck.

"Good to see you, Captain Arai."

"Well, well, well! Look who it is. I never thought I would ever catch the red-headed, rebel fan boy in the sky. Let alone with his own ship and crew. Looks like you're doing quite well for yourself!" Arai let out a hearty laugh and patted me hard on my back, nearly knocking me over."

"It does seem like so long ago, doesn't it?" I chuckled, trying to not show my nervousness.

Arai was one of the rebels I truly looked up to. I wanted to make the best impression possible, and not make it seem like I was simply playing dress up.

I pulled Faylin forward as if showing off merchandise. "This is Faylin, my first mate." I gestured to Lanker, who looked shocked before making his way over. "This is Lanker, my helmsman...and second-mate."

Lanker tensed and glanced over at me for a moment with a questioning look. But within a second, he caught on, putting on his best face.

"Second-mate, Lanker Barbosa, at your service." He bowed politely, winking at the quiet woman who was standing next to Arai.

She rolled her eyes.

Arai chuckled, walking closer, and grabbing Faylin by the chin. Faylin glanced at her but did nothing else.

"This is great craftsmanship; it must have cost a fortune. Where in Neutopia did you get this?"

"Well, Faylin and I sort of found each other. I agree, he is pretty great."

She let him go finally.

"I personally never liked humanoids. They always creeped me out. Looking human when they really weren't. It's weird. But, obviously, you've been doing pretty well for yourself. You're already making quite the name."

"Really, I would love to know what everyone has been saying." The sarcasm in that statement was a bit stronger than I meant for it to be. A part of me was a bit on the curious side.

"Well, you do have a nickname going around. Everyone has dubbed you, the Suicidal Scarlet. They're basically convinced you've lost your damn mind. I admit, I kind of agree with them. I mean, with the whole killing Salem's officers and broadcasting it to all of Neutopia, not to mention removing your collar. You got balls, I admit that."

Arai seemed more entertained than concerned. "Even King thinks you've lost your mind. But he's also very interested in your progress. The stupid old man can't even admit he's excited to see what you do from here. You're the hot new topic; everyone has their eyes on you."

I couldn't help the pride that swelled in my chest at that statement. Captain King, the most notorious rebel in existence, is watching me! He wants to see what I do next.

Everyone is watching!

My knees trembled in excitement; thankfully my coat hid it rather well.

"Well good." I cracked a smirk, trying to hide the red wisps trying to escape from my clenched palms. "I want them all to know, I want them all to see what we do from here on out. We aren't going to stop until Salem is dead, and I want them to know the name of the crew that made it happen."

Arai chuckled, the same fiery look in her eyes. "Now you're talking like a true rebel. And that's why I wanted to make you a deal. I want to help you, Scarlet. Or, I suppose I should address you as Captain Scarlet now."

The term "Captain" had never sounded so amazing.

"Of course, I would love to hear what you have to say." I shot my hand out towards my office. "Please, follow me. We can talk in my office."

Arai hummed in approval before following me.

"Of course, my first mate Stanislava and my second mate, Naii, will stay here and guard the bridge."

I nodded, whispering the same to Faylin and Lanker.

I opened the door for Arai, gesturing for her to enter.

Again, she hummed in approval as she looked around, pulling at my father's décor. "Vintage huh? This is nice."

"Yea, most of this belonged to my father. I tried to keep it looking...authentic."

"Very nice, I might have to take a few of these for myself." She glanced over with a dangerously amused look in her golden eyes. I chuckled before taking a seat in my chair, straightening my coat, making myself look like a captain.

I cleared my throat. "Now, what can I do for you, Captain Arai?"

She laughed, leaning back in her chair. "Straight to business, are we? Okay, that works for me. I have a proposition for you. Would you be interested in a mutually beneficial arrangement?"

Of course, the first thing I wanted to do was jump forward with the utmost enthusiasm. A chance to work with the infamous Captain Arai!

But I waited. I needed to handle this as a captain. And I can't let whatever she would say deter me from my goal.

"I'm listening." I leaned forward, chin resting on my face.

"If you are interested, I would be able to give you the coordinates of someone who you would find very intriguing. It would help you greatly. In return, I would just need you to do what you have proven that you do best. Understand me?"

"I understand, but I need more information. You're being rather vague."

It was a bit unnerving how unclear she was being. It was almost as if she was purposely speaking that way.

She made a gesture to the black collar around her neck with an aggravated expression.

I understood the gesture all too well. If certain trigger words were spoken, the ID number of the wearer is lit up on the census board. And when that person was found, it wouldn't be good for them.

Whatever Arai needed to tell me must've been sensitive enough that she was afraid of setting some sort of alarm off.

"I understand, and I want to hear your terms. Where can we talk about this further?"

Thankfully there were spots around the different regions that "temporarily" clouded the collar's signal. These zones were called "dark spots", and they typically were found in underground clubs or rebel-known bars. They didn't work for long, but it was good enough to get a quick word in without being sensed.

Arai nodded, pleased that I already knew the routine. An info-chip was slid over to me.

"Are you familiar with The Weeping Spirit?"

The Weeping Spirit had quite the name to it; an underground bar in the East, notorious for criminals and rebels alike. A very good dark spot in the rebel community.

I nodded. "When should I meet you?"

She stood, adjusting her coat and leaning in as she pushed the info-chip even closer.

"Tonight, midnight, Understood."

I nodded, a bit more enthusiastic than I wanted.

"Of course!"

She chuckled and held her hand out to me. I took it, shaking it respectfully.

"I will look forward to seeing you then, Captain Scarlet."

I followed her as she walked out. The scene on the deck was a tad bit tense. Faylin and Lanker were, more or less, right where I left them. Arai's two girls stood off to the side at full attention, not even speaking to one another. They eyed me as Arai and I walked out.

First mate Stanislava, a short girl with wild sandy brown hair, light eyes, and freckled skin that rivaled Lanker's. Despite her short and round stature, she held an expression that could freeze ice itself. Second mate Naii, a tall and statuesque dark-skinned woman who seemed to be Arai's elder by at least three or four years.

The left side of her body had been altered with bio-mechanics. Not completely uncommon, but still a bit unusual for someone her age. Everything from her left heel, up to her partially shaved head was decked out in shiny altered features. Her expression was a tad bit softer, she reminded me a bit of Faylin.

I was pulled from my thoughts when Arai turned back towards me, her glossy black captain's coat whipping, noisily in the wind. "I actually am glad I had a chance to see you again. I was hoping to run into you." She gave me one of her rare smiles. It was still a bit unsettling, but it gave me a sense of comfort.

"Me too, Captain Arai. I will see you tonight."

She nodded.

"Let's go you two." Arai hopped back on the bridge without sparing another glance. Her two crewmates followed suit. Just as quickly as they appeared, they were off into thin air.

I breathed out a breath that I didn't even realize I had been holding in.

"Geez, that was intimidating." Meeting her in the air, in her element, was definitely a lot more unnerving than seeing her after she had docked.

"A friend of yours, Mr. Scarlet" Faylin walked over, rubbing a spot on his chin. "She had quite the grip."

"I don't know Cap, she was pretty hot. I like the wild ones. Especially the one in the back." Lanker laughed as he came up next to me, leaning on my shoulder. "And...since when was I your second mate?"

I smiled sheepishly. "Well, it was kind of last minute. Do you mind the title?"

He smiled brightly, "Not at all! I'll wear the badge with honor!"

I smiled back.

"40 minutes until landing, Captain." Lanker bounced out of the room, full of energy per usual. But now, even more so, since his promotion. He had already filled everyone in on the ship of his new position.

I smiled, happy that he was so easily entertained.

I, on the other hand, was trying to hide my nervousness and churning stomach. Something felt off, and I hadn't seen R for the better part of the day.

Now would've been a great time for him to show up.

I was out of my usual attire, much to my disdain. Instead, I felt that something more formal would be better for the occasion of meeting up with Captain Arai.

A simple pair of fitted black slacks, black boots that had been shined to perfection, a stark white shirt with a striped vest, and a red tie that matched my hair and eyes perfectly. The entire ensemble was topped off with my freshly cleaned Captains coat. While I wanted to keep my hair in its usual tie, Faylin insisted on me taking it out and combing it. One of my least favorite activities.

It had grown even longer. When I had it out, it fell down my back, nearly hitting my hip. I knew Emme would be upset if I cut it, but honestly, a cut wouldn't do much good. Even as a child, father and mother would constantly cut my hair, and it would grow back within days.

Faylin took pity on me and assisted me in tying it back into a neat braid, and even smoothing my bangs back and completely out of my face.

When I looked in the mirror, I felt ten years older. I loved it.

It was thirty minutes before midnight as the ship landed in a wave of dust; Casteri met me on the deck, bringing the newly renovated T-34 with him. It looked exactly the same, except for a few additional pipes towards the bottom."

"Now Captain, even though you haven't had time to test this one out, you will need it for tonight and tomorrow. The safest spot for us to land was over fifty miles deep in the desert, so T-34 is the best way to travel. It still works the exact same way as before, but it should be more stable thanks to the extra CHEM running along the bottom. I already coded your DNA into the system, and it will only run if you are riding on it."

I nodded, approaching it like I would a wild animal.

I gripped my gloved hand over the handle and in one swift motion, jumped on as Marcus has done before.

For a moment, everything was stable. I took a deep breath.

"Thank goodness-"

A jolt ran through my hands before the T-34 jerked to the side, again, knocking me clear off.

Thankfully, I landed on my feet.

"How peculiar? I mean, I've heard of some people just not being compatible with hover-cycles, but never to this extent. Perhaps I could try something else to make it more manageable."

Casteri looked puzzled as I dusted myself off, giving a strained laugh.

"Don't worry about it Casteri, I honestly don't think I have enough time to wait around." The last thing I wanted to do was be late for Captain Arai.

"Understood, but, I can't think of another way for you to get there in time."

Thankfully, my favorite humanoid chose that moment to appear, clad in an outfit that mirrored mine.

"Mr. Scarlet, I might have an idea."

No more than ten minutes later, Faylin and I were zipping at breakneck speeds through the desert wasteland of the Eastern Region; Faylin piloting the T-34 without a care in the world, and me, sitting behind Faylin and clutching around his waist for dear life.

Every few minutes, I would feel the T-34 jerk in an attempt to toss me off, but Faylin was able to handle it, keeping it steady enough that I barely felt anything. Apparently, Faylin forgot to mention he was basically a professional at riding numerous types of hover-cycles. However, he refused to say where he learned the skill.

Faylin said he was planning on joining me at The Weeping Spirit anyway, adding in that he didn't entirely trust Captain Arai.

While I insisted on going alone, Faylin wouldn't budge.

It felt almost as if he was being more stubborn than usual. Like a passive-aggressive way of punishing me for not taking him up on his bonding offer.

I wasn't even aware that humanoids could be passive-aggressive.

But in the end, I needed him to come along to drive for me.

Humanoid 2, Captain 0.

With no more than five minutes to spare, the neon sign of The Weeping Spirit came into view. Per usual around this time, people of all ages hung around the rustic looking bar, chatting amongst one another. Loud techno music poured out of the smoky windows, though few people were dancing.

We pulled into the lot, and I hopped off quickly, straightening my coat.

A few people began to look, some in fear, others in confusion and suspicion.

"Are we ready, Captain?" Faylin came from the other side of me.

I nodded. As we walked, a few conversations began to resume.

Pride swelled in my stomach.

Another sound I couldn't pinpoint kept appearing, sounding almost like the crackling in a thundercloud.

It took me until we reached the doorway to realize it was Faylin's hands making the sound. The electricity was crackling at his fingertips; the sound was muffled when his hands were shoved into his pockets. His face was completely calm, but I saw as his eyes were taking in every single person in the vicinity. He wasn't just on guard, he was on high alert.

And he was ready for a fight.

"Captain Arai, glad you could make it."

After squeezing our way through and making it into the quieter back room, the woman of the hour finally appeared. And it seemed like Faylin wasn't alone in his suspicion, as Stanislava appeared in the background, giving me a dirty look.

Arai was out of her usual uniform as well, instead donning a formfitting bronze dress, along with her sword belted around her hip, and her Captains coat flaring elegantly. She looked stunning, but despite that fact, nobody tried to approach her. Her floral encrusted eye patch was enough to scare suitors off.

She eyed me with another one of her dangerous smiles, coming closer.

"And here I thought you weren't going to show up. I gotta say...you impress me, Scarlet."

She led me to a table near a back wall, shooing off Stanislava who nodded in response, taking a seat at the other end of the room.

"Your...first mate can stay with mine over there; we need some privacy over here."

I nodded at Faylin, signaling him to do the same.

He nodded back, heading over to the same table that Stanislava sat at. They sat silently, glaring back and forth at one another. I sighed, actually feeling less on edge with Faylin just across the room.

"Here, drink!" Arai slid a large glass in my direction. It contained some sort of bubbling liquor that smelled just as bitter as it probably tasted.

I feigned a smile as I pick up the glass, toasting with her.

"To new allies, and the guild."

She chuckled. "Fuck the guild." She clinked her glass against mine. "This...is to being real rebels."

She took a deep swig, slamming her cup down. I followed suit, trying to make the shiver down my spine less noticeable.

"Captain Arai, why did you think I wasn't going to come tonight?"

Arai sat back, arm hanging around the back of her chair.
"To be honest, I didn't think you would get this far. I'm annoyed
to admit I misjudged you." She glanced over at Stanislava for a
moment before continuing. "Most people nowadays, young and
old, want to be rebels, but they don't even know what the word
means anymore. They want to fly and be free from the thumb of
Lord Salem, but nobody is willing to make a move. Yea, a lot of
people talk big game about how they're gonna be top rebels, I
hear the same shit coming from little gutless townsfolk every
day, including you. You would smile and stare with those big ass
weird eyes of yours, talking about how much you admired King,
and all that shit. To be honest, I never thought you would ever
make it off the ground. You were too naive and innocent. I was
surprised you would manage to get to the docks on your own.
I played into your rebel fantasy because it was cute, and to be
honest, you didn't look like you had much more going for you."
I chuckled lightly. A part of me felt like I should've been
offended, but I honestly didn't feel that way. Everything she was
saying was the truth. Most people on the dock didn't bother with
me because it looked like something was wrong with me.
I guess most teenagers don't spend their afternoons staring at
empty docks, waiting for someone to show up.
Arai laughed as she continued. "I've known you for nearly six
years now, and it feels like you haven't changed a bit. But now
look at you. It's almost like you've transformed overnight. You
have a ship, a crew, hell you even have your own humanoid. You
were even smart enough to bring him with you tonight, and not
make an amateur move by coming alone. You openly opposed
Lord Salem and killed one of his officers, not to mention
broadcasted it still covered in blood. That alone takes more balls
then I have seen in the fucking guild. Not to mention you
removed this annoying thing."
She looped her finger around her collar with a grimace. "I've
been waiting for the right moment to take off this thing...but I

still haven't, and I've been doing this since I was a child. You have been in the air for less than a few months, and you have already changed the game. They don't understand what being a rebel is anymore. It's not hiding, and building barricades to keep the enemy at bay. It's taking the fight to the enemy, and not stopping until they are under our feet. And you and I, seem to be the only ones who understand what that means. So yeah, I misjudged you a lot, so consider this alliance a way for me to rectify that. I wanna see what you're really capable of."

I was at a loss for words when Arai finished. Was I that impressive to her?

I was almost afraid of saying anything, fearing any statement that came out of my mouth would make her take back everything she said.

Don't mess this up kid, be honest with her. Talk about Salem, stick to your mission.

I leaned in, hands folded on the table. This wasn't just a friendly chat sprinkled with blush-inducing compliments, this was a test. She was testing me, seeing how I would react.

She tested me to see if I would show up and if I would come alone, and now she's seeing what I would say next.

I focused on her.

Arai hated praise, and she hated being thanked. She saw that as signs of weakness. Her hands were relaxed but still tense.

While this might be a sign of her training, this also shows her level of relaxation. She is trying to appear to be relaxed, but she is on guard. Her feet are planted firmly and her hand is not out of reach from her blade. She's not relaxing around me because she doesn't only see me as an equal, she sees me as a rival. A rival with a common enemy.

The best option would be to play off her view of me as her rival, and not to show any hesitation.

I smirked. "I'm glad you see things the way I do. King is a great man, but I knew he wasn't the one who would bring Salem's reign to an end. I've been preparing for this mission for more years than I can remember. The research was nonstop, but I knew I had to strike hard and fast."

Arai's eyes glistened with mirth as she listened to me.

She was known for being one of the most ruthless captains around, so I would have to match that ruthlessness.

I continued. "My crew is strong, but even better than that; they have all accepted the reality they might not survive this mission. They are all fighting for their lives because they have nothing to go back to. That is why we are going to win. This mission might kill me, but as long as Salem dies next to me, I would consider that the most honorable way to go. So tell me, what can the infamous Arai of the Rusty Nail do for me?"

Dropping the "Captain" from her title was a bold and potentially dangerous move, but I needed to prove that I saw her as my equal now.

To my surprise, Arai laughed, downing more of her drink. "Very well played, Scarlet. I couldn't have responded better myself. I gotta know when did you realize I was testing you?"

I smiled, relaxing only a tad. "Come now, I can't tell you all my secrets Arai."

It felt almost unnatural saying her name so casually, but she seemed pleased with it.

"Well then, I believe you have proven yourself worthy of this information from me. I wasn't lying about what I said earlier. I am impressed with you, Scarlet. That's why I am giving this to you."

I nodded, waiting for her to continue.

She reached in her bag and pulled out an info-chip, along with a few papers. She slid the image towards me, face up.

The person in the image looked oddly young, with pale skin and unkempt dark hair. They were in a simple black button up shirt that went far past their hands, with dark shorts, high socks, and elegantly shined shoes. Their style looked slightly similar to Tyrinie's.

However, the most unnerving thing about their appearance had to have been the dingy white bandages that covered the better half of their face, covering the eyes completely. There seemed to be a larger person standing behind them, but the picture seemed to cut them out.

"Meet Nyx, Lord Salem's lackey in Sector 6." Arai leaned in, a twisted grin covering her face. "And what I want you to do...is kill this little cultist bitch.

END OF CHAPTER 16

17

DOWN THE RABBIT HOLE, AGAIN

❚ examined the image closer. Was this child really working for Salem? Were they the unknown Management officer in Sector 6? Then again, with everything we already knew about Salem's Hybrid serum, we had no clue what this child really was, or what they were even capable of.

My eyes glanced back at the tall figure in the background of the image, seemingly standing in the shadows. Nyx seemed to only reach their waist.

"Who is that in the background?" I scanned through the other images in the stack.

"That's Dante. Little Nyx's pet humanoid. That thing is downright brutish." Arai paused for a moment, staring down at her nearly empty glass. "I've seen more than my fair share of civilians having their heads bashed in from that thing. All Nyx has to do is nod, and he goes into action, not stopping until Nyx commands it. He's like some sort of rabid guard dog."

He certainly looked massive. Just his legs alone looked strong enough to crush concrete. Looked like he would be a bit of a challenge.

"Why are you giving this information to me? What is your history with Nyx?"

Arai glanced at me quickly, looking a tad bit startled, almost as if she didn't think I would ask that. There was obviously some sort of personal reason for this "request."

"I have my own reasons, none of which you need to worry about. This is something that benefits you, right? You're tracking these cultists down anyway." Arai's normal grin went right back to her face. "All I need is for you to make this one a top priority. After you're done here in the East, head straight to Sector 6."

Back to back missions would be tough. I didn't mind it, but who knew the condition the team would be in. Why was this, such a priority? There was something else happening here.

But perhaps I could use Arai's lack of patience to my advantage."

"Okay, in exchange for the information, I will take care of Nyx. That won't be an issue." I paused, leaning back in my chair.

"However, if you want it done so quickly, I'll need something else from you."

Arai rolled her eyes with an amused look. "Aren't you becoming quite the negotiator? Fine, name your terms for having this mission expedited."

I sat up straight. "Nothing I would need from you right this moment. My terms are only when the day comes that I attack Salem head on, I can count on your team to be there to back me up."

Arai froze in her seat, taken aback by the offer, before extending a hand to me.

"You have yourself a deal. Wipe that cultist outta my sector and my team will stand beside your team when you call us."

As if on cue, I felt as if Stanislava's eyes burned holes into my head.

As we stood from our seat, I took Arai's hand, shaking it politely before turning it over and placing a kiss above the ring on her middle finger.

I felt her tense up for a moment before chuckling. "Watch yourself, Captain, keep doing that and you're gonna get yourself in over your head."

Her cheeks had the slightest bit of red as she called her first mate over, Faylin followed suit.

I gathered the papers and info-chips as we bid each other goodbye. Another ally, another one up I have on Salem. Arai's crew was strong, and they held a lot of influence. This would definitely be beneficial.

"Arai" I called out to her before she left the room. She turned, quirking her brow. "Any specific instructions for this one?" I gestured to Nyx's picture.

"Just let me know when you're done."

I nodded, stopping only when Arai's voice continued.

"...and make sure that the little bitch suffers."

Faylin and I, mounted on the T-34, zipped back through the abandoned wasteland. It was nearly 2 am when Arai and I parted ways, each with a different load on our shoulders.

I wonder how Arai's crew will react when they find out Arai signed them all up to fight Salem with me. They would probably be pissed, but knowing Arai, she would squash any hard feelings then and there. There was a reason why she was one of the most feared rebel captains.

Unloosening one hand, I grabbed Nyx's file from my pocket, attempting to hold it steady in the wind.

If they had been pulled from the census, it must've been tampered with. There was no information, except for a few shots of them with Dante in the background.

What's even stranger is the fact that in each picture, they are facing forward. Almost as if they knew the picture was being taken.

The thought sent a chill up my spine.

"How much further Faylin?"

"Approximately ten minutes before arriving at the ship, Mr. Scarlet."

"Good." I nodded; I would need as much rest as possible for tomorrow. Another member of the Management was going to be destroyed, taking us another step closer to Salem. It wasn't only for my mission this time around, this was also for Faylin. This was so he could be free.

I couldn't help but ponder on what R had said to me a few nights prior. Something about how I would win, but it wouldn't go the way I thought or planned, like something was missing.

What was that supposed to mean?

My stomach churned.

"Mr. Scarlet?" Faylin broke the silence.

"Hmm?"

"Are you planning on truly taking Captain Arai up on her offer?"

I sat up slightly, still holding on tight. "Of course I am, I already promised. Plus, this will help us in the end either way. All Arai did was save us days of research. We were going to have to go after this one eventually."

"Yes, however..."

Much to my surprise, Faylin paused, almost as if he didn't know what to say next. The pause only lasted a moment before he finished up.

"This humanoid, Dante, his name is familiar. I believe if he is the same humanoid I believe he is, I might have met him before."

I shot up, nearly knocking myself off.

"What? You've met Dante? When were you in Sector 6?"

Faylin fell silent, facing forward as the ship came into view.

"That might be a story for another time, given as we have more to worry about at the moment with Dr. Plaski. But no, I had never met him officially. Simply...in passing. He is unlike any other humanoid I know. If you are insisting on keeping your promise to Captain Arai, we cannot go about it in our usual fashion. This would take a lot more."

A piercing scraping noise resounded as the hatch leading to Marcus and Casteri's lab opened, allowing Faylin and I entry.

I handed the notes over to Casteri. "I believe we found Management number 3. Some kid by the name of Nyx, along with a bodyguard humanoid, Dante."

"A child?" Casteri questioned, looking confused. "Honestly, I can't even question it at this point. I'd believe just about anything."

Casteri took a seat, popped on his glasses before taking the notes apart, bit by bit.

Marcus came from around the corner. "Hey Fifi, come here a sec."

Faylin nodded before excusing himself and heading over to Marcus' side of the room.

I headed upstairs.

I had been avoiding sending Persephone a message for a while. I know she must be concerned. With all of the talk going around about me, I can't begin to imagine what she must think. Or in the case, what Emme might think.

From the start, Persephone never knew about my purpose. I made sure that she never found out. She was never supposed to find out about my powers, but that came as a bit of an accident.

Persephone had no idea what led me down this path. In her eyes, I really had gone crazy.

Would she even return a message I sent?

I still hadn't gotten one back from the one that was sent days ago.

I closed the door behind me before grabbing the AT cypher.

Still no new messages.

I sighed as I began to type.

Mrs. P,

I'm sorry. There was so much about me that I should have told you.

I paused, not knowing what else to write. Should I tell her that it was all going to be okay? Or should I try and convince her I was a good person deep down?
Was I a good person?
I didn't matter, I was barely a person.
I sat back in my chair, poking at one of my souvenir water orbs and locking eyes with Myrah. This was why father tried to keep me away from humanity. I was destined to be different from them. I wasn't made to be a "good person." I just made them believe I was.
And boy was I a damn good liar.
I dimmed my lantern and laid in bed, still fully clothed.
The AT cypher beeped.
My message had sent.

I found myself sitting at the top of my family's staircase. Mother, Father, and Dr. Cain were all below, no doubt talking about me again.
I remembered this memory.
I had told them the men in red were talking to me, and Dr. Cain began doing all sorts of tests on me. But they couldn't understand what the problem was. I was a prototype; there was no control group to compare me to.
I stood, wobbly in my six-year-old body, and started to head down the stairs.
I didn't know what I was looking for.
Mother and Father came into view; they didn't seem to notice me. The conversation continued just as I remembered.
"Well, he'll be okay, right? We can't allow this minor blockage to destroy the whole plan."

I remembered hearing Father's voice like that, he sounded mad and also sounded scared.

"I'm sorry, but I don't know what R is trying to do to him. It might be harmless, but there is no way to know for sure. I'll keep looking. Don't worry, Lyrik."

Dr. Cain gave Father a reassuring smile.

It was like watching a movie. This felt as though it had just happened yesterday.

Mother stood.

I froze.

I had re-watched this memory so many times before.

Mother was supposed to stand and walk away into the other room. But instead, she stood firm, turning to Father.

"It's not like it matters, Lyrik. All we need is for him to live for 12 more years." She placed her hand gently on his head, brushing his hair back. "After that, he's not our problem anymore."

This wasn't my memory.

I felt frozen in place.

Mother continued to speak in the same nonchalant tone she used often. "He's too unstable since he's just a prototype. We all knew he wouldn't last long. Once he goes against Salem that should be enough to push him over."

Push me...over?

I looked over to Father; he seemed to have been pondering something.

"You're thinking too optimistically, Sabra. R-001 is strong, and he's getting stronger by the day. Thinking they will simply cancel each other out is insane."

"What makes it insane, Lyrik?" Mother crossed her arms.

Father sneered. "At the end of the day, Salem is just another humanoid experiment. He will never be as strong as an actual human. E-129 was damaged from the beginning. Damn that Xenon Tech."

Mother looked upset but hid it behind a coy smile. "E-129 was anything but damaged. He was perfection, which was the problem. Whether or not E-129, Salem, whatever he goes by is a humanoid or not doesn't make him any less powerful. Look what he has done already." Mother moved her hand from father's hair to the stubble under his chin. "And we copied all of that glorious power into the weak and unstable vessel of a human child. Trust me, darling, if Salem doesn't kill him first, the R-virus will. R knows that his vessel is weak."

Father began to laugh as he pulled Mother close. "If I didn't know any better, Sabra, I would swear you wanted R-001 to die."

"Well, I definitely don't want another Salem running around. You said it yourself. Just a tad bit more corruption and we would have more than one problem on our hands. Isn't that right, Scarlet?"

My heart jumped in my throat.

I slowly looked up.

All of their eyes were on me.

"I'm talking to you sweetheart. It's bad behavior to ignore your mother."

I tilted my head; the glassy window came into view. Emme and Persephone were staring at me, motionlessly.

Mother leaned in.

"I can see you, Scarlet."

I shot out of bed, sweaty and out of breath.

"Damn it, where's that lamp?" I flailed around the nightstand, bumping into my lantern and nearly shattering it.

The room filled with a blue glow.

I sat against the bedpost, watching every shadow closely.

"What...the hell...was that?"

I pulled my knees to my chest, it became hard to breathe.

My brain didn't know what to focus on. There was too much. I opened my mouth to call out, but...there was nobody to call. Nobody would understand what I was going to say.

I wanted to call for R. But those glowing red eyes were the last things I wanted to see. The thought of him watching me from somewhere in my subconscious mind didn't help me either.

I felt sick; my chest was too tight, body too stiff.

I turned my head, nearly jumping at Myrah's dull eyes. I wanted to leave the room, but I felt like I couldn't move.

I shoved the side of my hand in my mouth, biting down hard, drawing blood instantly.

Come on Scarlet, just focus on the deck, the war room, something. Anywhere but here!

I closed my eyes, feeling a familiar red halo circle around me. Within moments, I was on the deck, sitting on the hard surface, and staring at the beginning of a magnificent sunrise.

I think staying out here, for now, would be good.

When the first footsteps of life began to sound from below the deck, I stood up and stretched.

I lost track of how many hours I had been sitting. But I had refused to get up until I worked out what I saw.

My dream had been altered, or at least it seemed that way.

But, what if what I thought I remembered wasn't right.

What if the conversation from last night was the actual conversation? Nobody would know except for Mother, Father, and Dr. Cain.

And it wasn't as if I could talk to any of them.

Mother was against me, Father was missing, and Dr. Cain disappeared a long time ago.

But there were two things that stuck out sorely to me. The name E-129 was used as if it was interchangeable with Salem, and they mentioned him being a humanoid.

Salem, is a humanoid?

Why would they give a humanoid a nanoid? Was that even possible? Who was E-129 before he became Salem? Who did he belong to? And once again, the Xenon Tech popped up. What did they have to do with E-129?

Father and Mother, multiple times, said I was going to die.

No.

They said they wanted me to die. They wanted Salem and I to kill each other. I knew Mother wanted me dead since I was the only one who could kill her precious Salem. But father, why would he want me to...die?

I slapped my hands against my cheeks, taking in a deep breath.

It was a dream. It wasn't real. Father needed me.

I repeated the words to myself, like a mantra as my crew came up the stairs.

I forced a smile.

"Good morning crew, is everyone well rested for today?"

Tyrinie and Senna just groaned, walking past me, while everyone else said good morning. The only person I didn't see was Faylin, who was probably cooking.

"Well, I guess we can go ahead and eat, and then debrief over the plan for today."

Everyone filed downstairs while quietly chatting amongst themselves. As I thought, Faylin was in the galley zipping back and forth, laying out assortments of sliced fruits and fancy breads that he must've taken from the South.

Everything looked delicious, and everyone stared at the food. But nobody moved.

Faylin sat next to me, nose buried in his ever-present book. But every once in a while, a small greenish spark would hop off the page. His hands fought to look steady, but I could see right through it.

Marcus, who usually looked carefree, looked tired and worn. Of course, he tried to hide it behind his ever-present smile.

Lanker was oddly quiet, same as Tyrinie, and even Senna. Casteri was still looking over files that he carried with him. But even I could tell he was just looking over the same line over and over again.

I had asked Marcus to fill them in on the situation at hand while I was with Arai; to tell them about the hybrid theory, and the mad scientist who swore he could play God, and make immortal life. The only thing I asked him to keep from everyone else was the information about Faylin. That stayed strictly between Faylin, Marcus, and myself.

Everyone must've digested the true nature of the task at hand.

"I...don't really have an appetite, Cap." Lanker said, giving a half-hearted smile.

Everyone else groaned in agreement.

"Me neither, ugh." Tyrinie plopped his head down on the table, completely covered by his cloak.

This was a reality I had been taught day in and day out since I was a child. I knew this world was corrupted and on the verge of collapse. I knew Salem had everyone fooled into thinking they wanted a life like this.

Widespread Stockholm syndrome.

There were bits and pieces I didn't know. I never knew about Xenon Tech, I never knew about the Management.

For all I know, Salem could be a humanoid experiment, something created in the depths of Xenon Tech.

But I always knew one thing: that this world was going to hell. And it was my sole job to fix it.

But my team never knew this.

This was the ugly side of society nobody wanted to see, the side everyone wanted to ignore as if it was a story meant to scare children into submission.

They were facing the dark reality of where we live.

And I was the one who opened their eyes.

I looked around at my team. This was my team, and I needed to do something for them, to show them it was going to be okay.

I reached my bruised hand out for a piece of the bread Faylin had carved, the smell of honey and almonds wafted from it, making my stomach churn a bit.

I took a bite, humming in approval.

"You know, this is really good Fay! Where did you get this from?"

I smiled through the too-large chunk of bread in my mouth.

At first, Faylin didn't seem to even acknowledge my question until I kicked his chair, jarring his book from his grasp.

"I am pleased that you approve, Mr. Scarlet. I believe I obtained this from Madam Ginseng's brothel."

As I figured, Faylin stole it from her.

"What the hell?" Tyrinie shot up, cloak nearly flying off. "Are you insane, you can't just steal from Madam Ginseng?"

Faylin just shrugged, taking a sip of his drink.

"I don't know, Tyrinie. This is pretty good. If I was Faylin, I probably would've taken it as well." I chuckled. "What do you think, Lanker?"

I shoved a piece in Lanker's direction. He looked at me in hesitation, taking in my reassuring smile as he sighed deeply.

"Well let's see." He took the offered piece from my hand, taking a large bite. The freckled smile I've grown accustomed to finally popped up.

"I mean, this is good. I think stealing is justified in this situation." Lanker laughed, taking another bite before offering a slice to Tyrinie.

"All of you are insane." Tyrinie shook his head before grabbing a piece for himself. Despite the bitter words, there was a bit of mirth hidden there.

Soon afterward, the air felt normal again. Tyrinie and Lanker were going back and forth. Casteri, Marcus, and Senna were talking about their equipment and new discoveries.

Everyone was bonding over slices of stolen bread.

Faylin even seemed a tad less antsy.

Escapism and distractions don't solve problems. But, it was just enough to calm everyone's nerves.

The heavy stuff could wait until after breakfast.

Not long afterwards, we all stood in our uniforms in the War Room, looking at the hologram of the fortress that stood before us. This was unlike Myrah's fortress; there were no wings or different sections, just one large and sleek structure. There didn't seem to be any security, alarms, or defenses. Just a single structure, miles deep in the outskirts of the Eastern desert.

"Looks like our T-34s were perfect for this. Everyone else can travel via car. Would you mind driving, Senna?"

Senna shook his head. "That shouldn't be a problem at all."

I circled the hologram, taking mental notes. "There doesn't seem to be any other way in except for the front. Faylin, did you find an alternate way in?"

Since this was Faylin's previous home, I asked numerous times if he had any insight.

But according to his bits of memory, the majority of his conscious time was spent in the lab underneath of the fortress.

"Unfortunately, no, Mr. Scarlet. There is only one way in and out, and that is through the main entrance." He seemed sure about the statement.

I nodded, noting his eyes looked a bit lighter. When Faylin was focused, he was a serious force.

"Then it looks like we are going in head-on. Crew, this is just like any other fight in the past. And if anything, I'm glad we are all going in together, we will all be covering each other. We'll enter in a hexagram formation; I'll take front point, Faylin has back point, Casteri and Tyrinie will take left wing front and back respectively, and Senna and Lanker will take right wing the same way. Marcus, you'll be in the center for the time being. I'll need you to scan the rooms as we enter. Are we all in agreement?"

I looked around at everyone, and to my surprise, they all looked ready to go!

Lanker shoved his polished pistol in his holster, giving me a salute. "Second mate Lanker is ready for duty, Cap!" The others smiled, joining in his enthusiasm.

Dr. Cyryl was in for a rude awakening.

"Alright team, send the vehicles to ground level and file out. Let's show this bastard what the Seven Seas faction can do!"

"Rah!" Everyone filed out, scrambling in opposite directions.

Faylin and I remained in an eerie silence.

His nose was still buried in his book.

"Faylin, are you ready for this?"

He looked up slowly, focusing his eyes on me before nodding slowly. "Yes Captain, this will be an interesting battle, no doubt."

He paused before walking over to the doorway, turning at the last minute. "This is your last chance before we go into battle, Mr. Scarlet. Are you sure you do not want to complete the bonding with me?"

I nodded, feeling a chill. "I'm sure Faylin. I don't need to do that to you for us to win. I've got this, don't worry."

He nodded, heading out the door. "Very well, Captain."

I sighed, working out the knots in my arms, shaking off the pre-fight jitters.

"Anything to say, R" I felt his presence somewhere in the silent room, right out of my line of sight. No sound came. I nodded in the silence and headed out to join the others.

The dirt swarmed around in whips as the desert winds picked up. The sun itself felt like it could bake the few plants around alive. Despite that it was well into the cold season, the desert weather rarely changed.

Senna filed Tyrinie and Lanker into the back of the car, yelling at them to buckle in. Marcus and Casteri mounted their own T-34s flawlessly, mine stood untouched.

It was a tad embarrassing that I still couldn't ride one; nevertheless, I was thankful that Faylin was my willing driver, despite how weak it looked.

Faylin hopped on shortly afterward, hair tightly tied upward.

"Are you ready, Captain?"

I nodded, gripping onto his stomach, and settling myself on the slick seat, ignoring the laughs from Lanker and Tyrinie.

"Are we all ready, team?" Everyone raised their fist, and within a moment, we were a blur.

It took me a moment to catch my breath as we flew at breakneck speeds. Faylin handled the T-34 like a true professional. Marcus seemed to be able to rival that skill. Casteri, obviously rather new, lagged behind, but still managed to keep up.

I spotted Senna roughly a mile back.

He was probably afraid to drive above some imagined speed limit.

When the air moved this quickly, it felt almost as if the world stopped. The rush felt similar to when I would climb trees, like nothing else existed at the moment.

But something else did exist, and it plagued my thoughts.

Xenon Technologies the lab that started everything; It created CHEM, the first companion humanoids and according to my dream, created Salem.

The lab that was the scene of a buried massacre.

Why did that name keep popping up, and why did I still know nothing about it?

Whether I liked it or not, it looked like I would need to pay Madam Ginseng another visit once this was all over. I had a question that needed answering.

Are you ready for this, kid?

I froze as R filled my mind. I nodded.

Good.

I waited for instructions.

None came.

I was pulled from my thoughts when a large tower comes into view. No gates, no patrols, no overhead air traffic, just a barren tower. I saw as Faylin gripped the handles tighter.

"Full speed ahead!"

As more of the structure came into view, I noticed something that was out of place.

A garden grew outside of the doorway. Most of the flowers had wilted away, but many stood tall. Amongst them stood one particular one that made my hair stand on edge.

A sunflower, bright and golden, petals shimmering under the intense sun. I shivered and turned away from it, pretending as if it wasn't there.

We began to decrease in speed, stopping at the gravel walkway, desert tulips licked at our feet. This placed truly looked as if it might've been someone's home.

Faylin stared absently at the windmill that turned too quickly for comfort. The wind shifted as the others parked behind us

Senna parked shortly afterward, and once everyone was out, our hexagram formation was complete.

"Let's go, team." My sword was at the ready. I risked a glance back to see Faylin, his face was completely unwavering.

We approached the large doorway; I used the hilt of my sword to shove it open. It was unlocked; the room further in seemed to be lit by a light source in the far corner.

"I don't like this. Why would the door be unlocked?" Tyrinie whispered harshly. "It's like he's baiting us to go in."

There was no doubt something was amidst, but Dr. Cyryl was making a fatal mistake in luring us into his lair. This was just what we wanted.

I continued forward, prompting everyone to follow me.

Tyrinie hissed under his breath.

We continued down the darkened hallway, I felt the hair on the back on my neck stand on end. This darkness held a presence so heavy I could literally feel it on my shoulders.

The way into the next room opened up, and it seemed like some sort of study. CHEM lanterns hung in the corners, casting the room into an eerie reddish glow. Pictures, awards, and books framed the walls at all angles. But one word kept popping up. Xenon Technologies.

All of the awards were from Xenon Tech, and a man with stark white hair that nearly matched his lab coat, stood front and center in all of the photos.

"Isn't it grand to finally see you in the flesh, Scarlet?"

A shiver ran down my spine as a smooth voice appeared from seemingly nowhere. I pulled out my sword, the metal sound echoed loudly.

We all stood silently. I could practically feel Tyrinie trembling. The door behind us slammed shut.

"Show yourself, there's nowhere to hide!" I searched around, staying in formation. I couldn't let him separate us.

"Who said anything about hiding?" I looked in the corner of the room. There, in a deep red lounge chair, sat the doctor we had been looking for. His silvery eyes were enough to send a shiver through my body. His face was unmoving and stiff, like a mannequin. "My gracious, you look more and more like your mother each day."

I tightened my grip.

It felt like everyone seemed to know each other, and yet I know nobody.

"And how would I ever be able to thank you for bringing my beloved child back home, I was starting to think I would never see him again. All that research for nothing, I would have hated to start all over again."

Dr. Cyryl chuckled at my confused expression.

What research was he talking about? Faylin was made to replace his daughter, nothing more, so what research was needed?

"It's rather poetic, don't you think?" The doctor slowly rose to his feet, bronze cane in hand, the uncomfortable sound of static resounded throughout his movements. "Just as the prodigal son returned home, my hybrid mother has finally found his way back to me."

All movements shifted, the blood seemed to have left my face as I slowly turned my head towards the back end of our formation.

Faylin was gone.

END OF FILE 2

A Huge Thank You!
Sam B. and Diana R.B. for all of your kindness and help!
Chanell B. and Ashley N. for always keeping me motivated!
And my loving friends and family for putting up with me!

www.ingramcontent.com/pod-product-compliance
Lightning Source LLC
Chambersburg PA
CBHW020958180626
46814CB00003B/1153